Great
Textpectations

Ruchi Vadehra belongs to a family of writers from both sides of parentage. Writing is, thus, homecoming to her. She began with conceptualising and co-editing a neighbourhood community newsletter which inspired her to take forward her zest for words, people and travel, through fiction.

Ruchi lives with her husband, two children and family in New Delhi. *Great Textpectations* is her first book.

Great
Textpectations

Ruchi Vadehra

RUPA

Published by
Rupa Publications India Pvt. Ltd 2018
7/16, Ansari Road, Daryaganj
New Delhi 110002

Sales Centres:
Allahabad Bengaluru Chennai
Hyderabad Jaipur Kathmandu
Kolkata Mumbai

ISBN: 978-81-291-5183-4

First impression 2018

10 9 8 7 6 5 4 3 2 1

The moral right of the author has been asserted.

Printed at Repro Knowledgecast Limited, Thane

For my late father, Suresh Kohli

One

'*G*ive it up, Tarun! You can't be serious. There's enough happening in your story. It's busy; it's brilliant. It's got what it takes; don't add any more diversions to it.' Amaya tried to mediate with the writer sitting across the mahogany table. The meeting was proving to be quite taxing for her. She knew she was right and she wasn't about to give up her point of view. But Amaya also knew that the author, Tarun Bhaskar, was a toughie when it came to convincing people. He was unwavering.

'It's the missing link. I've spent days figuring this out. This is what will unsettle the peace.'

'Do we really need the "unsettling"?' Amaya asked, her voice laced with incredulity at the suggestion.

'Amaya, my work does *just* that. It causes disquiet. You of all people should know that by now.'

'I know your work is different; it's you. That is the sole reason it is at Amaya Books. That is precisely why you were rescued from that "mega" bad book world.'

'Ah! Lose the sales pitch, Amaya Kapoor. I'm already here for round two.' He pushed back his black thick-rimmed nerdy specs on to the arch of his nose and moved deeper into the comfy chair as if to indicate the conversation was over.

'That's not my point, Tarun. You had me at chapter one. But keep rape out of this, please! Why don't you understand that gimmicky controversy and sensationalism are poles apart? The former is a device that mediocre authors apply, not one as innately talented as you.' She moved forward with her hands firmly on the table—to indicate that this wasn't over.

'It's here to stay. It will work. All you need to do is see it my way.'

'You're being so cocky about this. Why don't you try and think about the other side of the argument?' Amaya continued, refusing to give in.

'Calm down. Don't throw a tantrum. Your entire office doesn't need to know what's going on in here.'

That did it for Amaya, she was furious. 'Asking you to give up on a bizarre and quite frankly, needless theory, is throwing a tantrum?'—she wanted to say, giving him a piece of her mind. Instead, she moved back into her leather chair and looked straight across the room. The painting on the wall made her inner peace genie take over every time she looked at it. She had spotted it quite accidently during one of her visits to an art gallery in South Delhi and had instantly taken to the Pakistani artist's work. It depicted the power of womanhood in a subtle way; the earthy hues imbued with just a touch of flaming red always sent calming energy to her. One look at it was pure anger management therapy.

She smiled benignly and said, 'Sleep over it, Tarun. I strongly suggest that you abort this "man on a mission" mode. It just doesn't work for you,' she added at the risk of sounding unceremonious. 'Rethink it, and so will I. Let's close it at that for now.'

She walked him to the door and took a few minutes to process the last hour. Phew! To think that no one had even known him till his last book.

She clearly remembered Tarun Bhaskar's maiden visit to

her office, five years ago. He had been chasing Mega Books, one of India's leading publishers, with no success. Complaining constantly about their unprofessionalism and apathy to the creative process, he had told Amaya that Mega had wanted to turn the basic premise of his book on its head. He had been quite clear that he wouldn't agree and Mega was not the right publisher for his book. He had then handed her a spiral-bound hard copy of his manuscript and pompously declared it would hold her attention from the very first line. Amaya had been struck by his confidence and unapologetic attitude. And what had truly amazed her was that his manuscript had her riveted, just like he had promised. She had wondered why anyone wouldn't want to publish it.

His second work was just as good if not better. For the life of her, she couldn't fathom why he would want to change a narrative that was such a flawless read, with every sentence in the book poetically in tandem with the author's incisive insights. However, she had witnessed many authors who started behaving like dickheads with just one bestselling title under their belts and Tarun was proving to be one of those. But she was determined; this time around, he would have to trust her instinct.

Settling her table and looking at the pile of manuscripts, she had a quick lunch and readied herself for a meeting with the design team. She looked forward to these meetings as they always charged her up. Titles and designs of three forthcoming books were discussed. The meeting became argumentative in no time. Amaya's suggestions were met with fierce protest from the younger lot. The word war went on with the thirty-five-year 'old' boss trying to add substance to the titles, and the twenty-something copy editors and PR girl trying to throw in 'catchier' ones. She loved the challenge. Working with a younger lot gave her a fresh and different perspective. Such sessions invariably concluded with a 'note to self' that experience via the chronology of age was not always a vantage point.

Promising to consider their suggestions, Amaya wrapped up the meeting and headed out of her Nizamuddin office to her kickass instructor aka soul sister Piya's yoga and Pilates studio in Greater Kailash. It was a sultry September evening. She needed to vent out her day by working out. Piya's studio was fashionably minimalist with wooden flooring, mirror-covered walls on two sides and floor-to-ceiling glass windows on the third, overlooking a tall, beautiful Gulmohar tree. The energy of the place both calmed Amaya's nerves and invigorated her. The time she spent here was more than a mere calorie-burning session; it was a spiritual connect with her version of 'God'. Here, in her quest to fitness, she disconnected with everything else and had a man/woman-to-woman chat with the power above. She had never been overly religious. Her upbringing did not endorse submission to any particular idol or religious belief. She had always believed that a prayer just needed to be earnest, no matter how it was chanted. Hence, Amaya would use this personal time to negotiate matters with the 'Almighty'.

For her part, Piya would ensure that the fitness routine was nothing less than a boot camp. What Amaya loved about the format was the customized version that maximized her workout needs. Piya's tall, slender and super-fit body could inspire anyone to emulate her method workout. Once in, Amaya would give it her all and more—sun salutes, total abs, stretches and finally, the breathing exercises. After the hour-long session, the two girls would bond over coffee every now and then—as they did that evening.

'What's with the aggression? You can't make yourself fitter, babe; stop killing it. What's the deal? A writer giving you heartache?' asked Piya.

'Heartache I can handle, Piya. But he's fucking my mind on a whole new level! I mean, his narrative's flawless; nothing needs to be touched. Out of the blue, he comes up with a brand new fancy and I'm not okay with that!'

'Maybe that's because he knows his stuff better than you do?'

'I don't claim to know it better. But I do know that what he's proposing now is not going to work. He's being such a bitch about this.'

Piya and Amaya had been close since school. They had stuck together through thick and thin—heartbreaks, drunken shenanigans, boyfriends, romances and then Piya's marriage. Atul and Piya had met while pursuing their B.Com in Delhi's prestigious Shri Ram College of Commerce (SRCC). Both had been on the high-powered MNC track but Piya switched to yoga post motherhood. They were the proverbial home-grown city couple, and Amaya was godmother to Piya's five-year-old daughter. Atul's job as senior vice president at a Fortune-500 company kept him travelling fifteen days a month but even then, the strength of their marriage was a reassurance to Amaya that in a world where breakups were the norm, there was hope after all.

Amaya's home was a thousand-square-yard construction in the uber-stylish Jor Bagh, a locality that had conserved its peace and quiet, a luxury not available to many in the capital. Taking in the smell of mogra, Amaya stepped into the sprawling living room overlooking the lush, manicured lawn that was her mom, Neena Kapoor's pride and joy. Neena was a landscapist and enjoyed dressing up the lawns in the homes and farmhouses of Delhi's rich and famous. Her own home exuded warmth and classiness, characteristics she lived to ensure.

The walls of the room were adorned with a large Satish Gujral canvas, Jatin Das watercolours, a pair of Raghu Rai black and white blow-ups, and several Lladró pieces strewn about. Amaya collapsed on the couch for a while. She was glad to have these moments of solitude; the absence of other members of the small family was a good thing in these times. The domestic help rushed in to ask if she'd like a drink; pushing aside the temptation of vodka as she was still mildly hungover from the previous night, Amaya opted for jasmine tea. It always worked.

With the Wedgewood cup in her hand, she headed towards the angular staircase that led to her room. She passed the den that had glass-lined cabinets and wooden shelves crammed with books. A stepladder was placed at the entrance. It was very much a book lover's house. After all, it belonged to one of the city's most well-known and respected booksellers—Amaya's father, Anand Kapoor. He was a man with humble beginnings who rose to become an icon in the publishing world by sheer hard work, showing scant bother about others' sarcasm when he would carry books on his scooter and move from one bookseller to the other. He had started Amaya Books thirty years ago in the heart of Old Delhi's publishing world—Ansari Road in Daryaganj—brushing the cheeks of Red Fort and the quaint but bursting at the seams, Chandni Chowk. The subsequent success he received failed to ruffle his modesty.

Amaya's last ten years with Amaya Books had been a good teacher and also a hard taskmaster. She had made a few bad calls, and at times let her emotions cloud her vision while selecting authors for the list. After having to sift through a multitude of the would-be, wanna-be, could-be and should-most-definitely-not-be writers, she could, by now, smell a good book from afar. Hence, it wasn't for nothing that Amaya Kapoor carried the often-admired mantle of one who had had fairly good success in identifying and bringing in a breed of young, new writers into the loop. She had made her entry into the Indian publishing industry immediately upon her return from London where she had interned in the editorial department of a huge conglomerate that had a number of imprints under its belt, thus giving her the exposure to a wide variety of genres including marketing and publicizing a broad list.

Amaya's hideout on the first floor was a self-sufficient zone. It had a pantry, bedroom, a sitting area and an adjoining terrace. On entering her room, she switched on the 42-inch television screen mounted on the wooden wall facing the queen-size bed. The orange and brown abstract-printed blinds on the huge window that overlooked the terrace were pulled down. Her room was done up in her favourite earthy hues, with low lighting, and always smelled good because of the fresh flowers kept in a Swarovski vase, a much appreciated gift from Piya.

She switched to a popular news channel that was booming with the voice of the belligerent newsreader. The ghastly rape incident that occurred some years ago in Delhi was news all over again. There was an outrage over a documentary by a British journalist on the unfortunate incident on one hand, and its subsequent banning in India, on the other. The trending topic was the comment of one of the rapists and his defending lawyer in an interview in the documentary. Each channel was trying to top the other's TRPs by picking on various related, and a few unrelated, topics. The comment was outrageous as the accused unashamedly blamed the 'victim' for her unfortunate fate. Nothing seemed to have changed in him in all these years. Far from accepting his heinous crime, he didn't even have an iota of remorse.

On another channel, Amaya watched the recently inducted

and extremely telegenic minister, Jyotika Narain. Yet another case of acid thrown on a young girl, occurring just after the rape case, was leading to a big hue and cry about women's safety in the capital. The minister, hard-pressed for answers by the bevy of aggressive journalists, was trying to escape the onslaught with the justification that she had just taken over, and needed time.

Watching all this, Amaya's resolve to convince Tarun to delete the new twist in his tale only got strengthened. The question was how. Thinking hard and trying to strategize, she stepped into the shower. Emerging in a cool cotton kaftan, with the television ramblings in the background, she made her way to the pantry. As instructed, the help had left grilled chicken salad and focaccia bread for dinner. She put the tray on the bed table and switched on her laptop. This was her favourite part of the day, when she unwound with online Scrabble—a pleasurable therapy and food for the mind. There were a couple of regulars she played with. She munched on her salad and browsed through the newsfeed on Facebook while waiting for one of them to make their move.

A 'Rohan Kashyap' started a new game with her. Playing with an unknown 'random opponent' was something Amaya usually refrained from doing. It was like entering unknown territory and Piya had often recounted the perils of gaming in the virtual world. With no other active moves to play, Amaya's finger hovered on her laptop while Piya's words resonated in her mind. What the heck, a thirty-five-year-old could very well handle virtual passes made at her. Besides, it may just be fun. There, key punched, and she was ready to lock words with a stranger.

While waiting for his move, Amaya checked out her opponent's profile. The photo looked quite all right. He lived in Mumbai; was single. Just then, a text popped up in the chat box, adjacent to the board.

'Hi Amaya, have a good game!'

'You too!'

She punched in and returned to her move. They played a few quick moves and then she made a 'bingo'—maxing points using all the seven tiles for her word.

He typed in.

'Ninety-five points! Way to go!'

She let it pass. And then, another message appeared.

'You're a pro. Been playing for long?'

'About two years now.'

'Cool. I got hooked two months ago. Very addictive, I have to say, especially if you have an adept player at the other end.'

'Yup.'

She hoped that her terse, monosyllabic answers would discourage him. There was an unspoken rule in the virtual Scrabble community—mind your own business, play your moves and avoid distracting side-chats. After a few more challenging and fun moves, she conceded that Rohan was indeed an able opponent.

'Timeout for me now. Continue tomorrow. GN.'

'Night.'

Amaya typed in her response.

Two

*D*amn! She was running late, thanks to an extended and never-ending meeting with a wannabe writer. That too on the very day she wanted time for careful consideration of wardrobe and accessories. A face-off with Meghna Roy called for it. Instead it would now be a quick stopover at home and an even quicker makeover. Donning a grey knee-length shift dress and a pair of comfy Espadrilles, Amaya touched up her face, and was off to the India Habitat Centre.

The red brick building, right in the heart of the capital, was Delhi's cultural and intellectual hub. The building, spread over nine acres, was dotted with lush green outdoor spaces, restaurants, banquet halls and the Stein Auditorium that hosted leading theatrical productions, and music and film festivals from all over the country and beyond. It almost always ran full house with those craving for a taste of stellar performances.

Amaya made her way to a panel discussion organized by Mega Books on a controversial new book that had just been published. A distinguished bunch had been invited to critique it. The venue was teeming with the familiar faces of the so-called Delhi literati and the hall was resonating with a husky voice Amaya knew well. She tiptoed in, glanced around and seated herself.

The head honcho of Mega Books, the big player of

publishing, and host for the evening, Meghna Roy, was seated in the centre on the dais with Jaideep Sharma, the author of the book in discussion; Shipra Shinde, the free-for-all-events activist; a familiar female model whose name Amaya couldn't recall; and the guest author, Tarun Bhaskar. Tarun was in his signature public-appearance look—a white kurta shirt and jeans with a black-and-white checked scarf casually wrapped around his neck. Amaya smiled to herself, thinking he looked every bit the cerebral, new-age writer.

It was a gripping debate. Tarun questioned Jaideep, highlighting how his book objectified women. 'How does a liberal like you justify this, Jaideep?'

The author jumped right in. 'The book isn't about me, Sir. Or my personal take on finding objectifications, objectionable.'

Tarun shrugged. 'In that case, let me rephrase. Do you not think that your protagonist, Inaayat, is shown in a regressive light?'

From then on, it was pure wordplay, with each panelist chipping in his or her two cents. Bringing the discussion to a close, Meghna Roy invited the audience for an interactive Q&A. Amaya was trying to stay attentive to the voices across the hall when Tarun moved the spotlight on her. 'Amaya Kapoor, you epitomize the smart, single, sassy Indian woman. What's your take on this?'

'I can't really comment on a book I haven't read,' she answered cautiously. Diplomacy was crucial in such occasions. She wasn't about to get sucked into the word war, especially when there was a huge chance that something she said would get misrepresented and flashed in the media out of context.

'But broadly speaking, do you agree that we, the *cultured* urbane, are a sexist lot?' Tarun continued, trying to bait her. 'Isn't that one of the points you are trying to make, Jaideep?

From a modern Islamic family, isn't your protagonist Inaayat dealing with the same issues?'

Jaideep nodded. 'Oh, absolutely.'

Amaya then knew she just had to interject. Caution be damned. 'The way I see it, sexism is just another form of racism. You can't divide it into urban or rural, rich or poor. Also, the tag lines attached to being single are not very flattering especially where it comes to women, though the same does not apply to men. Take, for instance, the term "sexually liberated woman". I mean, no one's ever heard of the term "sexually liberated man". That is a given, isn't it? But somehow, a prefix needs to be used for a woman to differentiate her from being...' she paused, 'a slut, for want of a better word.' Her impassioned words were met with generous applause.

She continued, 'All these labels and terms, alluding to a person's sexual choice and freedom, need to be done away with. We all know enough about Section 377. Homosexuality is a luxury enjoyed by the so-called elite, richer classes and celebrities. The lower and the middle classes have to pay a price for their sexual preferences. And more often than not, in gruesome ways that are beyond our imagination. I might be digressing here, but why must it take a rape case or lynching or stalking for us to wake up to "educating our sons" and "sensitizing society"?'

That said, Amaya handed over the contestation to the others who were keen to make themselves heard. From there on, she was just an observant listener, and of all the voices across the board, it was Tarun's that impressed her the most.

Post-discussion, the crowd mingled over wine and hors d'oeuvres. Tarun had two pretty young girls hovering around him. They started taking selfies on camera roll and he, albeit reluctantly, played along with them. 'Strange,' Amaya thought to herself, 'selfie is the new autograph in the Instagram world of this generation!' She looked around and her gaze fell on Meghna who was circulating among the guests.

'There was a time when I idolized this woman. I've learnt a lot from her. What to be and more importantly, what *not* to be,' Amaya confessed to Tarun, who was now beside her.

'She has quite a fan following.'

'Oh! She thrives on it. Meghna Roy can collect a crowd just by snapping her fingers. She's like the Pied Piper. They follow her wherever she goes. That's why you'll see so many regulars at all "Mega" events.' Amaya subtly pointed out to the Meghna loyalists who formed her entourage.

When she had made her formal entry into the world of publishing, Amaya had considered Meghna, over ten years her senior, a role model. The years that followed stood testimony to Roy's growth from strength to strength. She had worked her ass off to make Mega Books a pure reflection of its name. At the other end of the spectrum, Amaya saw her—an inspiring force for women in the business—fall head over heels for Sharad Verma, an ambitious young man who had started out as a mere copy editor in her company. Meghna Roy was oblivious to what was obvious to the entire office and she allowed Sharad to take over not only her mind, body and soul, but also build his stronghold over Mega. Meghna's husband, Abhijeet, became a bystander and even though he was 'officially' a part of Mega Books, he took the backseat in every way. Today, it was Team Meghna and Sharad that ran the publishing house.

Taking a sip of the red wine, Amaya said to Tarun, 'Anyhow, that interaction and your responses were electric! I hope you'll be as aggressive and passionate when it comes to arguments over your labour of love.' Amaya was glad to see that a number of people were congratulating him on his impassioned views. He was one for drawing attention as a writer, and both the woman and the businesswoman in her were pleased.

Tarun laughed, 'Well, you are the risk bearer and after listening to you today, I'm more than certain my work is in the right hands.'

'To think it almost slipped out of those very hands.'

'But it didn't. C'mon, so I seesawed a bit between the two of you. Am I never going to be forgiven for it?' Tarun pushed his glasses back on his nose, like he always did when peeved. Amaya recalled how Mega had tried to get Tarun back. It was something Meghna Roy wasn't going to either forget or forgive. Amaya Books had stolen this thunder from them and there was nothing she or Sharad could do about it.

Meghna walked towards them. She was nattily dressed in her favourite designer duo's ensemble, which Amaya surmised must have been custom-made for the event—a long, white kurta with subtle thread embroidery and flowing loose palazzos to go with it. The chunky neck-piece in contrasting semiprecious stones made just the right statement. Her waist-length hair was perfectly set and her attractive, botoxed, wrinkle-free face basked under the glow of make-up and success.

'Amaya, I'm surprised, pleasantly of course, to have you here this evening.' The two women air-kissed and then drew apart quickly, giving each other's outfits a surreptitious dekko.

'I wouldn't have missed it for anything. My star was centre stage,' Amaya responded.

'He's all yours now, aren't you, Tarun? Some steal that was, Amaya.' The air between them was tense and high-strung.

'You gave him to me on a platter, Meghna. I cannot be accused of poaching,' Amaya retorted with a cool smile.

'If only it was that small an appropriation!'

Amaya thought of letting that comment pass, but she

couldn't. Something about this woman always ticked her off, today being no different. 'Amaya Books doesn't pilfer. So, I claimed what was mine!' She looked at Tarun smugly. He seemed to be revelling as the obvious centre of attraction between the two publishers.

'You remind me of myself, when I was younger and shrewder,' said Meghna.

'You still haven't lost that touch, Meghna, rest assured.'

Before they could further lock imaginary horns, the media surrounded them. It was divine intervention. Amaya obliged with a random photo op, and moved to one side, allowing Meghna to hog the limelight. 'Meghna and I will always remain unfinished business,' Amaya thought to herself.

On her way back home, her mind reran the panel discussion and veered to the last few years in which Delhi had been a victim to gruesome rapes and racial murders. Almost each unfortunate incident had roused impassioned and aggressive reactions from both the plebeian and patrician populace; social, broadcast and print media had deluged with vehement debates and emotions running high; peaceful protests and candlelight vigils had made good at times, and at others, had turned ugly and violent.

Amaya's personal view was a tad bit different, even cynical. She thought it was just a matter of time when one occurrence died its natural death, making way to another for the headlines. This time, it involved a bizarre mother/sister-daughter/sister murder tale. The channels were relentlessly following the real-life drama, which kept getting murkier by the minute. Soon, another victim would usurp the country's attention.

It was late, and after three glasses of wines, she should have turned in, but couldn't resist getting on to the board. Of late, her peaceful Scrabble moments had found an exception in the form of Mr Kashyap. He was always up for a chat on the board with her. Unsurprisingly, just one move each into the game, a text appeared.

'There's a kind of comfort talking to you...feels like I could chat for hours.'

'We've only just begun. That was a quick conclusion.'

'But that's just it. You don't seem like a stranger...'

'Hmmm...'

Amaya typed in, a bit distracted while plotting her next move.

'Do you believe in destiny?'

'Yeah.'

'So, you too believe that there are no real coincidences in life?'

'We meet everyone for a reason.'

'That would imply that we were destined to meet?'

'Not too sure on "meet". Maybe our paths were meant to cross, can't say for how long though.'

'That remains to be seen. I'd say till Scrabble, do us part.'

'You are funny!'

'Why, thank you! Some ice is broken, finally.'

'Hey, I didn't mean to sound uppity.'

'Yeah, one never knows what young, single men may do to you on the Internet. The precarious cyberworld is full of stalkers, ain't it?'

It was as if he had read her mind.

'Well, you are my first "random opponent". I don't do this normally.'

'And to what do I owe this huge privilege?'

'I'm still figuring that one out.'

'Lady, you and your Scrabble moves are "safe" with me. Even if I want to, I can't walk out of the computer and into your room.'

'Yeah! That is probably the reason we've gotten so far.'

'This ain't "far", by far!'

'Your turn…and you're up against a bingo.'

'Damn! This is what happens when I get distracted.'

'That's why "chat less, play more" should be your mantra.'

'Or, it could be "enlightenment by the sagacious".'

'You're unstoppable, aren't you?'

'And, you finally see the real me!'

Amaya found him amusing and sharp-witted, always eager to make a conversation parallel to the game. She had taken a liking to that. His chats were quirky and he didn't seem to mind her tendency to philosophize, quite willingly accepting that she was older, hence wiser. Yet, she couldn't quite understand why a guy like him, living the assumedly single life, in a city as nocturnally alive as Mumbai, would spend nights getting to know strangers in the virtual world. What Amatya could fathom though, was that with every passing game, she was feeling less reluctant to chat with him.

Three

$\mathcal{T}$he three-storeyed building in South Delhi's tony Nizamuddin area was where Amaya was born. When the family moved base to their Jor Bagh residence eighteen years ago, Anand Kapoor shifted the office to this newer pasture. It was a sentimental move from Daryaganj, where it had all started for him. But it had to be made. Business was expanding and needed more space than the old office could provide. Many of his contemporaries still continued to operate from Ansari Road, and for many years after the move, Anand Kapoor returned to the haunt on Sundays, especially for the second-hand book market. Amaya accompanied him once in a while during her growing years, their common passion impelling them through the pathways laden with books. There would always be something in that treasure chest that would interest her and her father would indulgently allow her to add it to her shopping cart.

With a recent and much-needed makeover, Amaya Books was now ensconced on the second floor, leaving the two floors and the lawn below available to Amaya for her Project Bookstore. The plans were spread out on Anand Kapoor's desk.

After studying them intently, he said, 'I don't get it, Amaya. As far as I understand, you want to open a bookstore but the details here don't seem to coincide with that plan. Is this what is being constructed right under my nose?'

'Dad, why are you getting so hyper? Calm yourself down,' Amaya said, handing him a mug of fragrant and relaxing green tea.

'You do realize how easy it is to buy a book these days? One click and it is delivered at your doorstep.'

'That's just my point, Dad. This isn't going to be *just* a bookstore. "Amaya Books and More" will be an affair to remember; a haunt that people will frequent, something that goes beyond the regular format of walking in, buying books, grabbing coffee and cake, and moving on.'

'And just *how* do you propose to make that happen? It is five hundred square yards of floor space that is available to you. How are you going to justify its usage? I could just put it up for rent.'

'Both you and I know that you don't need rental income.'

'Be that as it may, I still need a proposal that works. By the way, what tea is this?'

'It's good, isn't it? Courtesy, Avantika Mittal—the latest entrant in the "organic" foods market. She's got this whole range going. I have my eyes on some of it, including the green coffee she's recently introduced. I'm working out the details with her to retail her products in the café. But I'll come to that later. Now, may I begin an informal presentation? So, within the parameters of a bookstore, there are three concepts in my mind. Concept one: "Author-meet". An author circulating with the footfall on an earmarked day. We could begin by holding the event once a month and then twice. We could even get authors in on the requests of our regular customers,' Amaya started off.

'I'm listening,' Anand Kapoor said, his neutral tone not giving away anything.

Amaya sipped the tea and continued. 'We've been in this for so long, Dad. Between the two of us, we can easily round up the writers. Just make them more accessible to their readers. Let them have a literary jamming session.'

'Are you not aware that despite "being in this for so long",' he air-quoted, 'how difficult it is to please these people? You want to be involved in feeding their egos at this stage in your career?'

'On the contrary, by now we know exactly what to "feed" to which writer. We know what makes them tick. In fact, some of the newer writers are sold on this concept,' Amaya went on in her efforts to convince him.

'What's next?'

'Concept two: A children's section where kids ranging from six to sixteen will be invited to the store to write short stories. We can run a workshop, fixed days and timings.'

'You and kids? When did that happen?' he teased her, well-aware that his thirty-five-year old daughter wasn't exactly child-friendly.

'It's a business move, Dad. And who knows? It might just activate my dormant maternal instincts.'

'Well, there are other ways to get your maternal instincts going, you know, the kind normal people rely on.'

Amaya ignored the allusion and continued, 'Coming back to where we were. An editor will be around to help them, maybe even an illustrator.'

'And what do you propose to do with these stories?'

'Simple. We select the best ones and publish the collection.'

'So, you intend to foray into unknown territory?'

'Yes, I intend to explore it and I think it's about time. Children's books have a huge market with immense possibilities. There's so much exposure for kids today. Reading is going downhill, with the internet and gadgets taking its place. How wrong could we go if we tried to channelize their interest in a fun, yet relevant way?'

'Okay, but then you need to keep these books entertaining, like you just said.'

'Exactly. That's why I want to publish the ones written by the kids. Go beyond storytelling sessions and book clubs. They've been done to death. The highlight is going to be the illustrations. The books will be so attractive that they'll be picked up instantly.'

Before he could react, Amaya quickly moved ahead. 'Concept three: A "reading room", where people can sit, relax and read.'

'Amaya, I'm running a business, not a non-profit organization.'

'Dad, just hear me out first. It's not going to be a thoroughfare. It will just give them a chance to choose what they'd like to eventually buy.'

'Not by the sound of it. It seems more likely that freeloaders will finish reading the books and keep them back, all this while lounging in Amaya's gracious library! How will you keep tabs? This is not making any sense, Amaya.' He paused and then continued, 'What else?'

'The café. I still need to work on what it's going to be like. It should be firmed up this month.'

'This whole project is going to go way over budget, Amaya. The different concepts will demand specific interiors; you're going to have to employ so many more hands than a regular bookshop. Salaries, outsourcing for the café.'

Amaya agreed that she would need extra budgeting, but she told her father she had a sense it would work.

'And have you discussed all the financial details with Akash to figure out where that "lot more" money's coming from?' Anand Kapoor asked, referring to their chartered accountant.

'I've had a couple of meetings with him.'

'Not good enough, Amaya. Your vision, your grand plans are all redundant if you don't give me a profitable situation to go along with it.'

'We can afford it, Dad. It's got to go beyond the math. It's my version of giving back to the society. You yourself have helped so many people become prolific writers just by following your gut. That's what I've learnt from you. And then, charity does begin at home, doesn't it?'

He shook his head. 'That premise isn't going to apply here. The way I see it, this is going to take up all your time and energy. How are you going to stick to your regular publishing schedule then? And if you don't do that job, be assured that there's no chance of there being any resources to fuel your bookstore. Also, if you try and alter the publishing programme, be well-aware that you are at a risk of losing shelf space in bookstores. You cannot afford to deviate from that, and then dealing with unhappy authors is an entirely other problem.'

'Managing my time is my responsibility. That should be the least of your worries. I have already put a plan in place wherein I will be working ahead six months instead of four on my manuscripts. That way, I won't risk any mismanagement of the schedule. As far as finances are concerned, and I truly appreciate your inputs here, if it comes to the crunch, I'll dip into my savings.'

'You will do no such thing. By the way, when was the last time you checked on your savings?' His tone conveyed his indignation. He'd got her; he always did when it came to this. Finance and Amaya didn't mix well. For all her gumption and fortitude, she found money matters taxing.

'Well, I'll figure it out.'

'By all means, do so. And while you're at it, get a reality check on your project. Work it out; make it feasible.' He made it very clear to her that the third idea wasn't workable and should be discarded. Amaya took his advice without an argument, though she was not entirely convinced. The conversation was then interrupted by a call from the receptionist, informing Anand Kapoor about the arrival of a senior writer.

'I'll do the best I can, Dad. But I promise you that Amaya Books and More will happen!' Amaya walked out even more determined than before. It was a challenge and she was ready to take it head-on.

Amaya scheduled a meeting with Akash for the next day. She tried to concentrate on the final draft of a manuscript an author had sent in but her mind was on the conversation with her dad. She went and stood by the huge glass window overlooking the busy road, akin to most traffic-laden roads in Delhi. Yet another bus had broken down, causing a messy jam. Damn, she thought to herself, it could take a long time for that to sort itself out. She hoped it happened before she stepped out. Deep in thought and observing the random goings-on, all she could think of was having all the project details figured out before her father got the chance to scrap it all together.

She returned to her desk and started her weekly assessment of the website. 'Looking good,' she said to herself and felt happy she had hired Radhika—a young fireball of a babe—to take over the site. She made a note to tell Radhika to work on the next add-on—a 'coming soon' header for Amaya Books and More. Wanting timeout to clear her head, she broke her 'no Scrabble during work' rule and moved to the board. Her latest opponent had played his turn half an hour back and showed up as soon as she played her turn.

'Do you work at all? Or is the main purpose of your life beating the world on the board?'

A text from him flashed.

'You got it! It is the bane of my existence, the fuel to my fire, my life's mission.'

'Sarcastic, aren't we?'

'Your comment warranted it.'

'Alright then, what else do you occupy yourself with?'

'Cheeky again, eh? I work…'

'And what work would that be?'

'Publishing books.'

'Ah! Nice!'

'Amaya Books, the answer to your next question.'

'I've read some of your books!'

'You read?'

'Gotta love your sarcasm. That would be an affirmative. *Sunset Diaries*, that was yours?'

'Bingo! On both accounts!'

'Back at you.'

He played a high-scoring move.

'Not bad. You're a quick learner.'

'I have a good teacher.'

After a couple of quiet moves, he continued the chat.

'Hey, don't take this the wrong way, but I'd like to get to know you better.'

'And…what might the right way be?'

> 'Hah! You got me again! Well, it's always fun to get to know new people and their perspectives on life…'

'True that!'

> 'So, what are your vital statistics?'

'Is this your definition of getting to know someone better? Men! Always so predictable.'

Amaya pictured Piya's face with the I-told-you-so look. Who in the world used pick-up lines like this anymore?

> 'Whoa, lady. Did you wake up on the wrong side of the bed this morning? Whatever happened to your sense of humour?'

'Pardon me, but vital statistics? Humour? Really? Downright cheap—no other adjectives can describe this get-to-know-you-better modus operandi of yours.'

> 'I should be the one begging your pardon. Not everyone can have an eclectic sense of humour like you, now, can we?'

'Condescending, are we?'

> 'Not at all. It's a genuine compliment. Okay, let's drop that question altogether.'

'While we're in the getting-to-know-each-other-better mode, let's hear it from you.'

She typed, wondering why she was even giving him another chance to counter his previous remark.

> 'Hold on! *You* want to know more about *me*? I can live without the niceties. You don't need to be patronizing. I've already rubbed you the wrong way by my "indecent" query, so give it a rest. We both know your

life will remain unchanged whether you know more about me or not.'

'If we're done with the drama, I'd suggest you play your move and give me a five-line introduction about yourself.'

'Rohan Kashyap. Twenty-nine. Mumbaikar. Single and always ready to mingle. Architect. Started my own firm, Cutting Edge, about a year ago; we take up urban housing and office projects, and we are now planning to enter the commercial arena in a big way.'

Amaya was impressed by the precision with which he handled the opener.

'Twenty-nine? That makes me retro.'

'And how so?'

'Dude, in today's time and age, every five years is a new generation.'

'Nah, you aren't retro. Take it from someone from "this" generation. You're pretty much out there. And now that it has been established that we both know we have to make a living, let's get back to it, shall we?'

There. It was over and out. He disappeared from the board as abruptly as he had appeared. She almost wanted to thank him. Being on the board with him was just what she had needed to switch off from her long day.

Neena Kapoor was relaxing in the living room, surfing channels, when Amaya walked in. A new political party had taken Delhi by storm in the elections. All the channels were agog with debates and discussions about it. Citizens were shouting out 'change' and 'hope'. Amaya plonked herself next to her mother, trying to concentrate, but her mind was on the conversation with her father. Her mother sensed she was lost somewhere, and turning the TV to mute, she looked at Amaya.

'Rough day?'

'Dad made sure it was.'

'I got a brief update.'

'So, I discussed all the ideas I had shared with you. Apparently, they aren't as kickass as you and I thought they were. And he had to bring up his favourite topic to get at me. He knows I can't handle money matters and he is right about that one! About time I get onto figuring the figures.'

Her mother reasoned and explained that all her father was doing was questioning the feasibility of the project. 'He's not wrong in doing so. You should use his experience and wisdom to your advantage. Just give it all another thought before making any final decisions.'

'I have thought this through, Mom. Look around the city. There is brand new and offbeat stuff happening every day. Clothes, food, theatre, art, you name it. I can't just sit around and let the world move ahead. We can do so much more with this store,' Amaya told her.

'And you will.'

'I've nailed it, Mom. I know I can't go wrong with this. Remember when I got back from London and told Dad to start publishing new and young writers? How reluctant he was!'

'He was but he did give you the freedom to find your ground. And you delivered then like you will now.'

Yes, her father had trusted her vision at that time. She had chosen to walk the less-travelled road by not tucking herself away in the comfort of the well-established business. She wasn't going to be just *any* publisher. She wanted to learn and then put into practice, the craft of creating a book from a raw manuscript. That's what her time in London had been for.

'What will be the USP about your bookstore, Amaya?' Neena asked her. 'You're emphasizing that you want it to be a unique space. So, shouldn't take you long to figure it out. That's the way I work. This is my first query to all my clients. Always. What is that one feature they need in the landscape that sets it apart? And the rest revolves around that concept.'

Amaya looked at her mother, admiring the clarity in her vision. Neena Kapoor knew it all, always did. Her life was the perfect balance of a working woman and the wife-mother combo. She had carved a niche for herself in her profession, choosing to work at her own pace and with people she liked. There was no place for compulsions when it came to the projects she took up or passed.

What *was* the unique selling point of Amaya Books and More? Why and how would it be different from all the other bookstores in the city? Amaya understood the point her mom was trying to make. She was almost there, in fact, she *was* there. The entire strategy would need to be reworked according to that one X-factor that would distinguish her bookshop from the others. She agreed that a reassessment of the entire plan would not be such a bad idea after all. The two then chatted about Neena's day.

'Not too bad. The Chhatarpur farm is nearly done. The clients are happy. I'm at peace. By the way, they have their eligible-bachelor son visiting them these days.' She winked at Amaya.

'Oh Mom, not again! As if one parent badgering isn't enough for the day!'

'Amaya, he's worth a look,' said Neena. 'What's the harm in just considering it? For all you know, he may be the one you've been waiting for.'

'No "looks" for me, Mom. And why do you think I am

waiting for anyone? End of discussion.'

Her parents tried not to show it, but Amaya was well-aware that deep down they wished their daughter would settle down. Like the way her younger sibling Anahita had. She questioned them time and again on their definition of the term 'settling down', because the way she saw it, she was adequately 'settled down'. The only missing piece in the jigsaw puzzle was a man. Yes, she could do with a partner in her life, but it seemed she could do without him too.

Amaya amused herself by thinking how her matrimonial ad would read. 'Thirty-five-year old female, wheatish to fair complexion, 5 feet 3 inches short without aid, between 5 feet 7/9 inches tall with aid. Slim built, worked-out physique. No natural beauty but attractive all the same, relies on the use of cosmetics to enhance her appearance. Sexually and mentally liberated; will cook and clean only for pleasure and leisure, financially secure enough to outsource the above services.' She wondered how many 'eligible bachelors' would give this ad the so-called look.

After a quiet dinner with her folks, where Neena did most of the talking about the politics of the day—a deliberate effort to maintain the balance amidst the chaos created by creative differences between father and daughter—Amaya retired to her room. Her mind felt like a dartboard, waiting for a 'bulls-eye'. Collecting the thoughts on her mind, she mechanically got on to the Scrabble board. Rohan had played his move and as expected, was his usual chatty self.

'That profile pic of yours tells me that you're hot and any man's dream babe. Then, why is *the* man missing? Just a harmless question. Please do not take offence to this one, or I'll give up my getting-to-know-you-better plan.'

'How can you tell based on one photograph that I'm the right thermal reading or that I am "manless"?'

'Hah! Another one of your gems! The latter is an educated guess. Well?'

'I still haven't found what I'm looking for, that should sum it up.'

'Talk about clichés! And I ain't gonna enter that iffy territory by seeking an answer to that one.'

'Iffy?'

'No ma'am, I don't wanna know what you're looking for. Women and their great expectations, and in today's age, even greater textpectations, completely psyche me out. Anyway, how does life move between the so-called single and attached stages? Many "good men friends" around?'

'Aah, by that you must be referring to "friends with benefits". The three magic words that do it for your demographic.'

'You're only five years ahead of "my demographic". Stop selling yourself as ancient. Anyway, you were saying…?'

'It isn't my kind of thing. I can live without the confusion such things bring up.'

'It's all in the mind. It does work, for most of us.'

'Not for me. I like to keep my "friends" strictly according to that definition. Tell me, you seem the bromance savvy guy. Would you do a male friend?'

'Where did that come from?'

'Exactly my point. It is that unthinkable for me to do a friend, male or female. Now you finally understand the friend zone.'

'I never thought of it that way.'

'So, my "friends" are allowed "benefits" of my company, loyalty and integrity, their gender notwithstanding. That's the way it works for me.'

'I have to say, I have rarely heard such a sorted version of relationships. The way you see things and the way you put them in perspective amazes me…truly.'

'It's just my perspective, and not quite necessarily sorted.'

'It is…at least for me. You could write a book with all your pearls of wisdom, you know, the *Chicken Soup for the Soul* kinds.'

'Except mine would probably be called *Vodka for my Soul*.'

'You're a wise one! My fractured soul's already on its road to recovery.'

'Your soul is fractured?'

'Isn't that the case with all of us?'

'Not really. But if that's your story, then you do need your soul to be worked upon.'

'Well, I have other areas too that could be worked upon.'

'I'm sure you do, but let's stick to soul therapy for now.'

'I'll take what I get. Maybe you can upgrade to the "other areas" by and by.'

Amaya wondered again why she was furnishing info bytes to a stranger. That he had her curiosity piqued was clear. He didn't question her motives or recent willingness to be more communicative. Instead, he just took it as it was and continued to carry on conversations from where they left. He surely had the knack of taking her into a completely different zone.

He continued.

'So, where were we?'

'On the board, obviously.'

'What kind of men do you like? That's where we were.'

'Last I knew, you didn't want to go down that road.'

'A guy can change his mind. It's legal, muh lady.'

'Sure, he can. He does it all the time. Like I said, predictable, thy name is man!'

'I plead not guilty. Don't write me off just yet. Coming back to you now. Your kind of men?'

'For one, I like men, not boys.'

'Okay! And what would be your definition of "men", Ms Presumptuous? Someone who's chronologically above the thirty-five age mark?'

'You're right. That was presumptuous of me, considering I live in a city where most men are boys.'

'Now we're talking. So, your men? How do you like them?'

'Like my coffee…strong, hot and stimulating!'

'C'mon. That's so clichéd.'

'Well, I did warn you that I'm dated. Not everything in life needs innovation and invention. Some things always work.'

'There you go again, your crystal-clear vision and zero pretension. That's what attracts me to you.'

'Attracts? You don't even know what I look like!'

'Is that a given too? I thought the wise ones see more in a person than what meets the eye.'

'Let's just say I'm not there with you yet.'

'Define "there".'

'"There" where I can take everything you say seriously.'

'I know better than to use pick-up lines on you. And, just to make it clear, that is not my intention with you.'

'What is your "intention" with me?'

'I find you refreshing, fun to chat with and someone who has the potential of becoming a friend. That's it for now. Don't flatter yourself by believing anything more!'

'This has got to be the first time I've gotten complimented and affronted at the same time.'

'And that would be the first kind word coming from you!'

Four

Piya's text read:

'Amu, be ready by nine. Dress super hot.'

'Define super hot.'

Amaya texted back to her pal who was her self-appointed wardrobe consultant. Piya's fashion sense was very 'with it'. She was a follower of the fashion capsule and did so with complete finesse. Amaya, on the other hand, had never been one to fall prey to fashion trends. She liked to dress in a way that was uncomplicatedly stylish, basic and comfortable. Piya's love for 'colour' was in complete contrast to Amaya's monochromatic hues that crammed her cupboard. That was why the double check about what Piya had in mind always helped.

'Virat HOT, I'm thinking the short black number you showed me the other day. Nine then.'

Piya's retort flashed with a winking emoticon.

So, a short black tube dress it was, with hair worn long and straight, face done up with a base, smoky eyes laden with kohl, a nude lipstick and her current favourite Prada fragrance. Super-high black heels, the Ferragamo black clutch and she was good to go when at a few minutes past nine, her phone beeped, announcing the arrival of Piya and Atul.

'Virat's got this location bang on, huh Atul?' Amaya asked, sinking back on the plush backseat of the Porsche Cayenne.

'Yeah, he's at the right place, at the right time, as always. In the high life, living his dream. He just knows the pulse,' Atul lauded his buddy from school.

'He's truly God's chosen one. Everything he touches turns into gold,' added Piya.

'Virat Bakshi, the new age metrosexual, swag-oozing, mojo-working male. Gourmet restaurateur, successful businessman, with his rags-to-riches dream run, the charisma—he's a man hard to ignore,' Amaya said rather speech-like.

'Hear! Hear! The la-di-da Amaya Kapoor's ode to Virat Bakshi; perfect opening lines for his memoir, which I'm sure he'll write soon enough. A real success story,' Piya added.

'Who knows? Maybe Amaya Books will do that for him,' Amaya said.

'And for all you know, there might be a chapter in it titled "Amaya",' Piya retorted playfully.

They were headed to Meherchand Market, or Khan Market Part-2, as Amaya liked to call it. In the last few years, this spot had metamorphosed as an extended arm of urbane Delhi's leading shopping and hangout spot—Khan Market. It was now an area dotted liberally with couture shops and speciality restaurants.

As they got off the car, Atul glanced at Amaya's shoes. 'Amaya, the "Fuck Me's!" What's the plan tonight?' he asked with a glint in his eye.

'It must have been a really vain arsehole who came up with this whole "fuck-me shoes" bull. A man won't look at my face, boobs, ass, walk, or garb. But one look at my shoes and he'll guess whether or not I plan to get laid this evening? So, if I wear flip-flops, then I guess I'm PMSing!' Amaya scoffed.

'It's no wonder men don't need to don such indicatives. They're ready to get laid anytime,' Piya added. Atul was lost for words with the two women who clearly had him ambushed with their witty rejoinders.

'GREEKY!' read the headboard outside the restaurant. The font, resembling the Greek alphabet, was white plaster of Paris against a blue background. They stepped into the strikingly done-up modern Mediterranean abode.

Team Bakshi—Rupali and Virat—were putting their best foot forward. The event was trademark 'Virat'—flamboyance overloaded. Delhi's leading DJ was in the house, the bar was laden with exotic alcohol and well-turned-out waiters were doing the rounds with hors d'oeuvres.

The hosts walked towards them, Rupali ahead of Virat. She greeted Amaya while her husband turned to give a big hug to Atul and another warm one to Piya. He waited till Rupali was out of earshot, busy chatting with Piya and Atul. Sidling up to Amaya, he scooped down, keeping his peck on her cheek and arms around her waist a tad bit longer.

'Amaya, it's been a while! You have a knack of disappearing every now and then.'

'Isn't that the happiness of pursuit, Virat? I hide and you seek me?' Amaya looked at him, straight in the eye.

'I try, I do try. But you don't make it easy at all,' he said, placing his hand on his heart in mockery.

'But you don't like "easy", do you?' she continued.

'You got me on that one,' he answered, looking right back into her eyes. 'I like a challenge, always.'

'And I aim to please.'

'Cheers to the chase then.'

'This is a neat place,' Amaya changed the subject smoothly. 'The textured white walls, the flooring, the authentic upholstery.

Cool stuff. What are these photographs that are put up?'

'They make a statement, don't they? I'm glad you noticed. Most of the crowd here can't see beyond the free food and drinks!'

'They're hard to miss.'

'Got a Greek photographer to capture these. They're a mixed collection of various Greek islands, all originals, by the way.'

'You don't believe in cutting corners, do you?'

'Nah. It has to be perfect, always. Be it my work or my woman.'

'The latter I wouldn't know about...' she shrugged.

'You could, if you wanted to. By the way, I'm gonna be camping here for the next few weeks, what with these soft launches every second day. Need to handle teething issues and all kinds of customers. Don't want them going viral about shoddy treatment, blah. So, I could do with some company. Come over anytime. Tea, coffee, a drink; I'm available too, just so you know,' he said with an inviting wink.

'I'll keep all the options in mind,' Amaya played along.

'Gotta go, darling. But you hold on to that thought,' he said and dashed off.

The presence of shutterbugs confirmed that the event would make it to 'Page 3' of the leading dailies. Piya and Atul were mingling with the quintessential Delhi couples floating all around. Amaya had neither the desire nor the inclination to be a part of that crowd right away. Their discussions about domestic staff and kids, and the other gossipy ones about 'who was sleeping with who' bored her to death and she had nothing to contribute to except monosyllabic 'hmms' and 'aahs'.

She made her way to the bar. It was a relief to be able to catch her breath for a few moments sans company. She sat on the bar stool and sipped on an iced vodka drink, garnished with a slice of lime and diluted with soda. She casually began observing the couples hanging around on the cool white sofas, moving to the beat of the music, guzzling alcohol, showing off their diamonds, their conversations probably revolving around the millions they had accumulated, recounting holiday destinations and how socially connected they were. These were the very people Virat had probably hinted at earlier in their conversation. It was easy to get typecast in this city, and it was so convenient to be one of the many. Then there were others, like her, vagabonds, not wanting to confine to the herd, always trying to find a way to migrate to the fringes.

'Amaya? Amaya Kapoor?' a husky voice snatched her out of her thoughts.

'Raina? It's Raina, isn't it? You look so different!' Amaya exclaimed.

'But you look just the same. The long gorgeous hair, super fit body.'

The two women hugged each other.

'How long has it been? Ten years, easily?' Raina recollected and Amaya agreed. That was the last she had heard of her college mate. The woman standing before her was different from the one she had known. Her curly hair was longer and she had gained noticeable weight. The once bright and radiant face seemed to have toned down with the addition of years.

'Let's step out for a smoke,' Raina took her by the hand and they walked out to the patio. She lit herself a Marlboro and offered one to Amaya.

'I quit three years ago,' Amaya said.

'*You* quit smoking? And to think, you were the reason I took to it.'

'Those were crazy times…' Amaya reminisced. 'So, what brings you to Delhi?'

'I'm back for good, babe. After twelve years, the single life again.'

'Didn't work out? Prince Charming turned back into the toad?'

'Worse! He found himself a Prince Charming!'

'Oh shoot! But everything had seemed alright on your trips back home.'

'I thought so too. Didn't last too long.'

'And?'

'Shit happens, babe. You see it around, hear it happening all the time. But somehow, you live in a bubble, thinking and believing it can't happen to you, until it does. And then…boom!' Raina stubbed the cigarette and lit another one.

'True that.'

Marriage, its façade, meanderings and overrated sanctimony were eternal pennies to Amaya's thoughts. She asked Raina about her work.

'I've picked up a job with *Notebook Delhi*. Nothing spectacular but it's paying the bills; putting my life into a routine until something better comes along. What I need right now is stability and sanity.'

'And here we are, forever finding ways to beat the monotony.'

'Believe me, I've done crazy, and it isn't always as good as it looks.'

'So, what is it exactly that you do at *Notebook Delhi*?'

'Unearthing unknown elements and vistas of Delhi, this multifaceted city, along with covering all its goings-on. What's working in my favour is that the city has a lot happening. Delhi has so many layers, quite like an onion. Every time I am out to explore the city I discover something mysterious, something exciting. It keeps reinventing itself in so many ways. I'm doing a piece on Meherchand this week. Got a whiff of this place being launched and here I am. Who would have thought this rundown locality would get wings? We didn't even know this sleepy area existed.'

'Yeah, to use a cliché, it found its calling.'

Raina then asked Amaya, 'So, how are things with you? Amaya Books? Gautam?'

Amaya hadn't heard that name in a while. 'Amaya Books, yes. Gautam, no.'

'No way! How did that happen?' Raina asked in complete disbelief.

'You're not the only one shit happened to,' said Amaya with a smile.

'Hmmm...seems we have many years to catch up on.' She stubbed her second cigarette and said, 'Let's go back in. I need a drink.'

They walked back into the cool indoors and spotted Piya and Atul. 'And I was just telling Atul that maybe the shoes seem to have worked! Where did you disappear?' Piya whispered to Amaya and moved her focus on Raina. 'I know you...' she added, trying desperately to place Raina.

'Remember Raina? My college batchmate? English Honours?'

'Oh! Yes! Yes! Of course. Been a while!' said Piya, a wee bit embarrassed.

'Refills everyone? Let's drink to renewed ties. I'll just make a quick dash to the restroom.' Raina excused herself. Amaya filled in Piya about Raina.

Rupali joined the two ladies. She was wearing an electric blue, embellished floor-length gown and silver stilettos and seemed to have walked straight out of the MAC store, her eye shadow matching her gown. Her hair was coiffured, so as to make sure no one missed the colossal diamond and rhodium chandelier earrings. 'You both must taste everything on the menu. And give me a frank opinion on what's good and what's not. The menu is my responsibility; Virat made sure of that. Babe, we've really been working so hard to make this place authentic,' she said.

'The place looks every bit Greek. Good job, Rupali. The only thing missing is a tanned Greek God!' Amaya said, tongue-in-cheek.

'Oh, Virat fills up that spot!' Rupali then gushed about her 'amazing husband' and how he managed to do it all. It was more than obvious that she was in total awe of him, or rather, the man he sold himself to be. The hypocrisy of these so-called perfect husbands, who never missed an opportunity to satisfy their roving eye, was yet another 'man-thing' that Amaya never understood. Who would believe that the same Virat—the devoted husband—would give another woman a second look? But that was the real truth, and Amaya had first-hand experience.

'The support of our friends is what we need. It keeps us going. Please try the souvlaki. It's going to be our house specialty,' Rupali said.

Raina returned just as Rupali moved off to socialize. She downed her drink rather quickly and said to Amaya, 'Virat Bakshi. I've been following him and his tweets for a while. The man's got the power all right. His wife though, I can't figure the match. What's the story there?'

'Not much, except, some mismatches are made in heaven too!' Amaya replied. 'They're a crazy-in-love couple all the same.'

'Ha ha ha! Good one, girrrllll!' Raina slurred.

'Raina, you all right?'

'Couldn't be better. Let's do a round of shots! Vodka shots, I say! Hey you, Mr Bartender, three Grey Goose shots, now!'

She passed the shots to Piya and Amaya.

'He's hot, babe. So fuckable,' Raina said to Amaya with her eyes focused on Virat.

'Hey, you might wanna take it easy on those shots,' a miffed Piya warned Raina. Piya wasn't one to mince her words.

'It's Saturday night! And I've just reunited with my long-lost pal. That's reason enough to live it up. No, you aren't the one who's lost, Amaya...that would be *me*!' Raina drawled. 'I'll tell you a secret, Amaya. I haven't done it in like a month now. And that isn't good for me, babe.'

'Ummm, do you wanna tell her how long it's been for you? Maybe that'll sober her up,' an amused Piya whispered to Amaya.

'This is your moment, Piya. Revel in it,' Amaya allowed the joke at her expense.

'VIRAT! VIRAT!' Raina called out and drunkenly walked towards Virat who was engaged in an intense conversation with Atul. She faltered on a step and squatted on the floor right in the middle of the restaurant. Atul rushed to her and tried to get her on her feet.

'Raina, c'mon, up,' Amaya too walked over to her. She put Raina's phone and other scattered things back in her purse.

'I can't, Amaya. My foot! It's hurting like hell! Amaya! I can't get up!' she said and burst into tears.

'Amaya, she's totally wasted. Let's get her out of here before this gets any more embarrassing,' Atul said. He got the staff to help and lift her. At the other end of the room, Virat was desperately trying to pacify an overwrought Rupali.

'We need to take her to the hospital,' said Atul. He waved a goodbye to Virat, who understood at once what was being conveyed to him.

'Do something, Amaya. My foot, it's hurting like crazy. Get me another shot, it'll numb the pain, it always does.' Raina was oblivious to where she was and what was going on. Ignoring her desperate pleas for another drink, they got her into the car and headed straight towards the nearest private hospital. Screeching to a halt outside the Emergency Ward's door, Atul jumped out and ran off to call a couple of attendants who then helped Raina onto a wheelchair.

'What a sight! Walking into a hospital at one in the morning with three skimpily clad tipsy women! I feel like a bouncer!' Atul said, half-laughing.

'Correction! Two now no-longer-tipsy and one completely wasted woman,' said Piya.

'Piya, she's not going to sober up by your repeatedly calling her wasted. She doesn't even know where she is,' Amaya said.

'Where are we, Amaya? Is Virat here? Hey, you bartender, where's my shot?' mumbled a delirious Raina.

'That's a doctor, woman. What are you on?' Piya was livid. She found such behaviour rather obnoxious as she had never been the kind to completely lose control of her senses. Enjoying a drink was one matter and making a spectacle of oneself publicly was quite another.

A young, smiling doctor attended to them. Atul informed him about Raina's fall. 'Let's see what we have here,' he said and began examining Raina's foot.

'Ooh! That feels good,' Raina said to the doctor.

'Sorry, please excuse anything she says,' Piya told the doctor as plainly as she could.

'Amaya, this guy, he's so frigging hot. I wanna do him now,' Raina went on. Thankfully, the doctor was out of earshot by then as he had just turned away to talk to a nurse.

'What's with her wanting to "do" every man on the planet?

Are you sure she hasn't chased her shots with something else? Check her bag.'

Piya had guessed it right. Amaya fished out a strip of pills and showed them to the doctor when he returned.

'Hmm…these are anti-depressants, and it is more than likely that your friend has popped a couple. That would probably explain her state. Nothing too harmful. She'll sober up in a few hours, once the effect of the alcohol starts wearing off.' He added that her injury was, in all likelihood, a ligament tear but he could confirm that only after further examination. Raina had no idea what was going on and continued to gaze longingly at the doctor.

'I'm sure you're used to much more than this, Dr Aditya,' Amaya said in her feeble attempt to downplay the embarrassment.

'Part of my job, ma'am. We see so much happening around here, it's best to keep calm and carry on.' Raina was wheeled inside for an X-ray while Amaya, Piya and Atul waited outside.

'It's late. And there really isn't any point in the three of us hanging around here. You both get home to Kaira. I'll take care of this,' Amaya said turning to Piya and Atul. Despite their vehement protests, she insisted on taking charge. They didn't need to be a part of this crazy drama any more.

'How will you get home? And Raina?' Atul asked, concerned.

'Please tell me you're not thinking of adopting her!' Piya said to Amaya, sounding somewhat freaked out.

'Not if I can help it. I'll call her folks, and drop her off to her house. I'll figure it out, Atul. You guys get going.'

'Are you sure? One of us can stay. This really isn't your problem, Amu.'

'It's not. But we have a situation and I'll handle it.'

'Okay, but call if you need help.'

'Of course I will. Piya, don't worry. If she acts up again,

I'll just leave her with the doc,' Amaya said with a quick wink.

'Amu, you're hilarious!' Piya added, giving her a hug.

After they left, Amaya called her driver to the hospital. She then pulled out Raina's phone—which thankfully wasn't password-protected—from her bag, and found a number listed under 'mom' in the contact list. Raina's mother recognized her instantly. Steering clear of a detailed account, Amaya said that Raina had hurt her foot and she was bringing her home. While Raina's foot was being bandaged, Amaya cleared the bills and thanked the doctor. She then helped Raina into her car, instructing the driver to first head to Defence Colony.

Raina's house looked nothing like it had ten years ago. It had gone through a complete makeover. Retirement seemed to suit both Raina's parents. She greeted them warmly and after taking Raina inside with her dad's help, she gave them an edited version of the events before heading home.

Amaya hit the bed as soon as she got home, but kept tossing and turning, the events from before running through her mind. She was desperate to get some shut-eye but the vision of Raina's state didn't let her. Snapshots from the past and the present oscillated in her mind.

Raina—the image of her puffing cigarette after cigarette—transported Amaya back to college. The two girls had bought their first cigarette from the *paanwallah* near college, had hailed an autorickshaw and had coughed their lungs out during the ride. Soon, it had become a pack instead of the one or two odd cigarettes and the exercise went on till they got it right. The kick of the nicotine surging in her body, the liberation she had felt. The South Campus girls' college—English Honours classes, hanging around in the canteen over endless cups of tea and planning their life ahead. How had USA made Raina the person she now was? Tonight, she had been a mess, amiss and completely out of control. Drink after drink, anti-depressants, vodka shots, and the blatant concupiscence. Something was not adding up.

Gautam—how Amaya's world had revolved around him. He'd wooed and charmed her till she had fallen head over heels for him. He would be there to pick her up from her college almost every day and the two would chat for hours in nearby discreet locations or at times, in his Maruti Zen car. The stolen kisses and the ineptness and inelegance of the first time they had sex; the contentedness and assurance of being with him; the thrill of an orgasm; the sex being a declaration of their love and commitment; them sneaking into her place while her folks were away; making out; making love; her bribing Anahita to keep her secret safe—the memories came rushing back.

Anahita—her baby sister—had become her closest friend and confidante and the five-year age gap between them had all but disappeared. She was with Nikhil, now in the USA. It hadn't taken Anahita long to decide that Nikhil was the one for her. And off she had trotted, leaving only memories behind.

Piya—who had since been her pillar of support— was Amaya's 'go-to person', one who was there for her unconditionally. She had kept her sane after Gautam. She recalled how Gautam had gotten into IIM-A for his MBA and she had left for London for two years. She'd taken off on a whim, knowing that she could join her father's company right away. But she had wanted to 'evolve' into another Amaya, see the way the world looked at publishing and bring back more to the table for Amaya Books.

In her state of half-sleep, Amaya got hazy visions of how different her life would have been had London not happened. Near-forgotten images flashed—her pleading to Gautam to trust their relationship, her resisting all male attention in the idealism of monogamy. Her returning to India, only to find out that he had become a changed man.

'I have to leave, Amaya. I can't be in this country anymore.'

'And I can't leave. You know that. You've always known that.'

After having spent six years together, after making it amply clear to him that she had to be at Amaya Books, his sudden apathy to it all was crushing. The inevitable break-up, the trauma, heartache; picking up the pieces and traipsing back to life. Thank God for Amaya Books. It had been her Mecca; it had given her just what she had wanted at that time—solace, long busy hours, direction, diversion, new opportunities, and new people. The void and the gaps got filled with her work. Piya and Anahita—her two rocks had been by her side and had helped her edit Gautam out of her life.

Amaya's mind then rushed to their meeting five years ago. Gautam was getting married and wanted her to be there. How, in that weak moment, he had grabbed her hand. 'There can never be another Amaya. I've missed you. If only I had done it differently.'

'And your point being...?'

She had made the statement coldly, bereft of any emotion. It was clear to him that she had moved on. She was over him. She was over the melodramatic Bollywood drama her life had almost become. She had refused to attend the wedding, a carefully taken decision. She had decided she was no longer going to give in to impulsiveness.

The dance in the trance returned to the present and another image from the night came to her—the women who had been there at GREEKY. She could have just as easily been one of them! She almost had. She had narrowly escaped that predicament when she had refused the marriage proposal from the son of her dad's best friend. He had just returned after completing his education at an Ivy League university and had joined the family's thriving export business. Living at the right address—Aurangzeb Road, the habitat of Delhi's wealthy and influential—the smart, but overtly snooty dude had told Amaya that he was a forward-thinking modern man. Of course, she could work with her dad, but not at the cost of sacrificing the social and domestic demands of a married life and also only till the time they 'started a family'. Then she would 'obviously' have to devote all her time to the 'kid' and could do some designing work for their company to keep herself amused. Or work part-time with her father. He stated confidently that he was sure her father would understand.

'In the same way perhaps, as your father would understand if you worked part-time, for your own business?' she had asked him cheekily. He didn't get that Amaya Books was as much a full-time job as his would be. He couldn't comprehend the comparison, and that was the end of the story that never began.

Her mind moved to Piya when she had been undecided about Atul and she had convinced her that she'd lucked out by finding him. Atul was dependable, mature and wise. Men like him didn't come by easily. She would perhaps not mind a man like him. Some more visions of men passed by—the ones that had floated by, with not even a single one able enough to retain her interest for too long. Except, maybe, Virat.

Virat and Rupali, Virat without Rupali. His sheer persona—those eyes filled with ambition; the determination to win on all accounts; the eloquence of his flirtations. In all this, she saw the vision of Amaya Books and More—her dream that would soon become a reality. And amidst all the assimilation, slumber overcame her at some point.

Five

Amaya sat at her desk the next morning, pondering over the forthcoming titles. Of the four new books, she was certain at least two would cross the twenty-thousand print run. The advance orders from the distributors had indicated that she would need to plan for a quick reprint. The thought that retailers awaited titles from Amaya Books was indeed comforting and reinforced the fact that she was on the right track.

Glancing at the bejewelled Vacheron Constantin that sat snugly on her wrist she realized that Tarun was an hour late for their meeting. The thought had just processed itself in her mind when he walked in.

'I don't have all day, Tarun.'

'Sorry! I just lost track of time.'

Not wanting to waste another minute, she came straight to the point. 'So, I take it that the whole victim-victor addendum to your story is history?'

'Amaya, the way you say it, it really does sound corny.'

'Well, that is because it is. You can't just marry off your writing with a random episode on a whim.'

'Yeah, I guess I am just overwhelmed with the pathos of the situation.'

'You want to contribute, figure out a plan that's more compelling.'

'True that. Anyway, I am going with your gut on this one.'

'Then trust it. Your book is going to cajole the reader to turn the pages. Three options for the cover—take your pick. This one's completely on you. A final reread, the sign-off, and we print!'

They started going over the designs on her laptop when Tarun finally said, 'I'm going for the third one.' His decision made Amaya smile.

'Yet another golden moment, Tarun! The writer and the publisher are on the same page.'

'There's no debating this, Amaya. This one belongs to *The Love Unaffair.*'

'So, that's sorted. Now, let's shortlist a couple of excerpts as teasers for the book.'

'Oh no! Perish the thought! Even thinking of having my book up for sampling of any kind is loathsome to me. Buy it or borrow it, and of course, the newest, deplorable option— download and read it. But I'm not going to give away excerpts of it. It will be akin to selling my soul. Amaya, I am an old-school writer. A traditionalist. I believe some things are sacrosanct and must not be tampered with.'

'I knew the agreements wouldn't last long,' Amaya shrugged. 'The excerpts are going to happen, Tarun. You need to embrace these changes. Give the reader a tease.'

'It's a book, Amaya. Not an aerial view of a cleavage. The "tease" is irrelevant.'

'I know it's a book and not a cleavage, Tarun! The comparison is odious.'

'My bad. That was a tawdry metaphor.'

'It certainly was. That said, and coming back to where we were, what is so revolting about giving your readers a snippet or two? There isn't anything unacceptable about it. Treat it like the various tweets you put up.'

'Not the same thing.'

'It almost is, just an extension of bits of the book on social media. It's the way forward and keeps you connected with your readers.'

'I feel it intrudes upon my privacy as a writer.'

'They are going to be reading parts from your book. We're not taking them into your bedroom, Tarun. Don't mix up the two elements. And stop being elitist about this.'

Tarun shook his head; Amaya couldn't make sense of it. *The Love Unaffair* was a winner; anybody with half a mind would know that. Planting excerpts was crucial and why it was inviting acrimony from her author was beyond her. She was, however, hopeful that in due time, Tarun would see reason and agree, as he had with her earlier suggestion.

On his way out, Tarun said, 'Hey, I'm having a few friends over this Saturday. Do join us if you don't already have plans.'

The invitation caught her unawares as she had always maintained a candid yet professional relationship with Tarun. Socializing with him had never crossed her mind.

'Uh, okay…sure.'

'Great. I'll text you the address. Saturday then.'

From one clever one to another. This one was a number on the Scrabble board and he lit up her mind in his own whacky way. He was the only one who had made her break the rule. She couldn't resist playing with him every once in a while during work hours. She could do it—switch on and off in limited time.

'Hey, you up for a quickie?'

A text in the chat box parallel to his game moves was a given by now.

'Huh?'

'Chill! I meant a quickie on the board! Let's wrap this one up…got some time to kill if you do.'

'Depends on how "quick" you make the moves.'

'What's the time window we're looking at?'

'Thirty to forty, max. What's with the time to kill?'

'Got a few interviews to run in a couple of hours…wanna stress bust! What better way to do so than give a brainy lady a run for her money… BINGO! This one's mine, btw.'

'Not so soon! Back at you.'

'You're good at this!'

'You'll get there too…just a bit of patience and practice. That always works.'

'Yeah…I'll get there…just patience.'

'Whatever! So, what are you hiring for?'

'This and that. Wanna apply? I am always eager to get services.'

'Depends on what you're hiring for. I am very selective about what I offer.'

'There are many areas of specialization that I can think of. For instance, you're good at these quickies.'

'Mr Oh-so-cool, the only place you're going to be offered quickies from me is the board.'

'Yeah, I do know, and believe me when I say thank God for small mercies! Damn. This is getting serious now. I hate to lose.'

'You sound like one who does. Too bad, wise guy, you've got to learn to take the fall somewhere. Where's your sporting spirit? Gone kaput?'

'I'd show it to you in other ways than on the board, if you so desire.'

'I have no doubt about your sporting abilities. I like to play the game differently though.'

'Aah, as long as you like to play, I'd say we have a good thing going.'

'See, this is what happens with hot-blooded blokes. You lose focus and there, boom! Ends your dream of victory.'

'Nice. Thank you for being with me. Keep in mind that I'm hiring for services. See you on the board soon.'

Six

It had been a week since Raina's disastrous night-out when Amaya dropped in to check on her.

'Limping back, quite literally! I know you have a lot of questions, Amaya. And I owe you explanations, especially since I dragged you right into the middle of the mess that I am,' Raina said with the slightest of drawls she had acquired from her stint abroad. They were sitting in Raina's bedroom, sipping coffee.

'We can talk about it another time, Raina. As long as you know where you stand and where you need to go from there.'

Amaya wasn't too keen to get into any details at that moment.

'I do. But some days, I just succumb to being the person I had become. And then, I get jolted back, realizing even more that this isn't who I want to be anymore.'

'That's half the job done. Look, I am not going to judge you. But there are things you said that night which require some thinking. Take your time. And when you're ready, we'll meet over a drink and talk.'

'You still want to risk meeting me in the company of alcohol?'

'Why not? It's still the "shit happens" phase. You need to tide over the tough moments. They'll pass, but only if you let them.'

'Believe me, I am trying.'

'I'm sure you are. Just keep at it. You aren't going to get any sympathy votes from me. But, for everything else, I'm just a call away. We aren't getting any younger, Raina, and are mature enough to know and understand how to figure out our lives and not blame our issues on anything or anyone but ourselves.'

They chatted for some more time, catching up on the years gone by and agreeing that a lot more heart-to-heart conversations were needed. But that's the thing about some relationships—more often than not, they can be picked up from right where one had left off. Raina and Amaya were in that place.

Being a thirty-five-year old single woman in the city, one just gradually gravitated towards the flock; and that's exactly what had happened with Amaya in the last five odd years.

Barring the few constants, the post-thirty graph had seen her stocktake the people in her life. She had effortlessly drifted away from those she didn't share the same wavelength with and had cemented bonds with the ones that vivified her mind and provided her with comfort and happiness.

In the process, she had hand-picked a coffee klatch. They were eight of them, between twenty-five and forty, who met once or twice a month over coffee and conversations. They also watched plays and movies; hung out and got wasted—depending on what the need of the hour was. The maverick outlook of the gang struck a perfect balance in Amaya's life, against the 'other' lot, the thought processes of which were far more institutionalized.

Though Amaya got along with all of them just fine, two, in particular, were closer to her heart—Mihir, thirty-nine, a freelance photographer and Noor, who was twenty-eight but believed herself to be far more mature than her age group and thus, chose to hang out with this gang.

Mihir was all Amaya could have ever asked for—independent, self-made, erudite with a whacky sense of humour; they had hit off almost instantaneously when she had met him five years ago. It was expected that the two of them would become the proverbial 'couple'; but in spite of all the ingredients being perfect, this recipe could not make a gourmet dish. Now, they both continued to be each other's inner voice-cum-partners in crime. Noor was the wild child in the gang. She was sprightly, full of zest and had been trying her hand at art, sculpting, and her latest passion—pottery. Mihir and Noor existed in the 'fuck buddy' zone, a relationship status that was suitable to both of them.

They had all gotten together at Hauz Khas Village, a party hotspot that had some rocking pubs. Amaya used to hang out there regularly during her college days as it had a popular nightclub and interesting dining joints. The Indian fashion scene had just about found its feet and HKV, as was its fashionable abbreviation, was where most designers had their outlets. Then all of a sudden, the area had gotten erased from Delhi's nightlife and entertainment map. Remaining dormant for a while, it had resurrected itself to become a hub of cafes, specialised eateries, fine dining, stand-up comedy shows, and performances by musical bands. With the backdrop of the lake and Mughal architectural ruins, HKV made for a great location for an evening out for many.

The pub where the group met was hugely overrated in Amaya's opinion. It was overpriced for the quality of food it offered. It was owned by a popular restaurateur and was well-publicised. She couldn't get what it was that made people cascade here. The place made her feel old. The bulk of the crowd was in their early twenties. She sighed to herself, watching them guzzle away alcohol. But she wasn't old! That's what her Scrabble pal Rohan would say. Remembering a text conversation she had recently had with him, she turned around to ask Mihir, 'When you ask a woman what she wants in a man, what do you expect her answer to be?'

'You mean, any woman or *you*?'

'Let's say both...'

'That's forbidden territory, Amaya. No man can provide a near-satisfactory answer to that question, and hence better sense prevails in completely circumventing it.'

'That's exactly what he said!'

'Who?'

'Uh, just someone I'm on the board with.'

'Random someone?'

'Yeah, sort of. He said quite the same thing you did and he's about ten years younger than you!'

'Then he's smart and has figured out women early in life!'

'Hmmm...' Her mind strayed to Rohan's absence from the board the last couple of days. She had gotten used to his noisy, but thoroughly entertaining, company, that to her surprise, she was now missing.

The rest of the gang joined them and they were soon exchanging notes on work, relationships, hook-ups, parent-pressures, dreams, aspirations; too much sex or too little of it, legit and illicit affairs, and mundane everyday details.

'Oh! To be in love like that!' Noor sighed, seeing a couple on the dance floor.

Sitting at the rooftop bar gave the guests a panoramic view of the city lights. The live band and people's high-pitched chattering voices were reverberating all around.

'I give you love like that, babe. Only, it's more horizontally expressed than vertically,' Mihir winked at Noor and turned to Amaya.

'You in the mood to burst her bubble? You'd be doing her a favour.'

'What bubble?' Noor asked.

'Oh, nothing,' Amaya replied. 'Just a practical joke I used to play; we called it "the real love test".'

'No way! And why is it that I've never seen you take this test?'

'Honey, I don't take the TEST! I prowl and conduct it on preys that succumb to it,' Amaya said with a sexy drawl to her voice.

'Bring it on then,' Noor was ready.

Amaya focused her gaze on a couple on the floor, more steadily at the guy. She held up her glass, took a swig, all this while looking directly at him. The guy suddenly noticed her advances and within minutes, he swung his girl in such a way that he was now facing Amaya.

'There you go. Step one!' she told Noor.

'What did he just do?' Noor asked, catching onto the game.

Amaya ran her fingers through her hair, locking eyes with him between her conversations with the rest of her gang—a secret audience to the drama. The man's attention was largely towards Amaya, who was totally involved in the part she was playing.

'Noor, keep talking. You don't want to give Amaya away,' Mihir warned a fascinated Noor.

'What a jerk!' Noor downed her drink.

'There's more to come,' Mihir added.

The girl on the floor whispered to the guy; he nodded and she walked away. Not losing another moment, he walked up to the bar, very close to the gang. Amaya continued to give him the 'come hither' looks and raised her glass. He beamed and reciprocated the toast. In no time, he moved close to Amaya; Mihir slipped away to give more intensity to the drama.

'Cheers!' the guy said to Amaya.

'Back at you,' she smiled.

He was shifty, and Amaya was well-aware of that. The Delhi man's awkwardness and inadequacy at opening conversations had always exasperated and amused her at the same time.

Act Two. His partner returned from the ladies room, and he gestured to her to come to the bar. He got her a drink and propped her on a bar stool, keeping Amaya in direct vision, only even closer now. Within moments, his dearest caught onto the goings-on and the party was over. There was a powwow, the lady seething, her man trying to calm her down. They walked out of the bar, and then, curtains call. Noor was befuddled at the drama that had just unfolded. She went outside for a smoke and was soon joined by Amaya, Mihir and a couple of others.

'What you just saw was Amaya's rendition of the age-old concept of a tease, with a 100 per cent success rate!' Mihir said and held onto Noor.

'I hereby crown you Goddess Amaya, and I stand before you sadder and wiser!'

'Don't look so heartbroken, babe. That was just one bad egg,' Amaya tugged at her affectionately. 'Let's not give up hope on that "one perfect man" just yet.'

'Something tells me you've found a basket full of them over the years.'

'Yeah, I've had my share of collectables.'

Mihir kissed Noor and told her to lighten up, and soon, she was totally into and onto him. The lighthearted, relaxing evening came to an end, and they all bid goodbye to each other, rejuvenated to deal with their respective tomorrows.

Seven

*F*ollowing her resolve to be well-versed with her money matters and not leave it for her father to handle, Amaya had a few meetings with the chartered accountant. It did not take her very long to get her head around the finances. This was followed by her giving the entire project a rethink and Amaya agreed to meet her dad halfway. So, the reading room was done away with and replaced with a reading lounge, a smaller area with comfortable seating, tucked away between the bookstore and café. The 'author meets' would take place on the upper floor that would also accommodate the children's section. Now that the placements were decided, she moved to step two of the project that comprised dealing with the interiors and furniture. Amaya had been surfing various sites and studying bookstores, apart from having discussions with the interior designer. She wanted the bookshelves to be designed uniquely, while the 'author meets' area needed to have an aesthetic literary setting.

Amidst all this, it had been another Rohan-less Scrabble week. She was left wondering why someone so active and overenthusiastic on the board would suddenly vanish. It slowly dawned upon Amaya that she was hooked to this 'virtual boy' who made her time on the board a thrill ride. Her phone buzzed. There was a message on Facebook Messenger. Rohan!

'Sorry, messaging you out of the board. Hope that's cool. A lot happening at work so may not make my moves as often as I'd like to.'

'Hmmm…so you'd rather make the moves off the board?'

'Aah, you get the drift…finally!'

'I'd rather you made them on the board. Lots of fun to beat you.'

'Don't count on it. Gonna be back soon and avenge myself.'

'Is aggression your middle name?'

'Oh yeah! And totally worth it on the board. I hate to lose.'

'Haven't I heard that one before?'

'Wait and watch, lady! Anyway, just wanted to drop a "hi" lest you wrote me off!'

'Yeah. Later, then?'

'Just too much going on, can't commit to when later.'

'Hey, it's a conversation, not a marriage proposal. Don't need a commitment!'

'Phew! Thanks! And since we've levelled up on the communication mode, feel free to impart your pearls of wisdom…they kinda make my day.'

'You got it.'

Yes, she was hooked all right. Amaya had never imagined that this could happen to her—that someone she had never met would take a place in her life.

'That new move today, the butt kick? What a burn!' Amaya

told Piya. She'd had an intensive session and was refuelling her stamina with an energy drink.

'Yes, it's a fusion between asanas and aerobics. It alters the muscle movement for better and more result-oriented impact.'

'It better! It's a killer when it comes to my stamina. Another plus to your "good pain" series.'

'It will. You need to do it twice a week, minimum. We'll replace the lunges we were doing with this one.'

'I like this new pattern, Piya. The flow from one exercise to the other; it's rhythmic. You should keep reinventing. It makes the whole workout super challenging.' Amaya took a sip of her drink and continued, 'By the way, Tarun's invited me for dinner. Saturday night, his place.'

'Tarun? The hot writer?'

'There are other adjectives that can be used to describe men. FYI, he is a non-looker, short, nerdy, with a nothing-to-flaunt physique. The only part of his body that works for him is his mind. All the "hotness" probably resides there.'

'That works too, doesn't it?'

'Not always. But nonetheless, the evening should be interesting. At least I hope so. Never thought I'd see him beyond work meetings.'

'It'll do you good. Hey, how's the virtual man doing?'

The mention of Rohan brought an involuntary smile on Amaya's face. 'The virtual mystery man; he resurfaced after more than a week.'

'You guys chatting often?'

'Off and on.'

'What do you chat about?'

'Anything, everything. He's so quick on the uptake. He gets things even before I've said them, rather typed them.'

'It's weird, Amaya. For two people who haven't even met,

you do have a lot to talk about.'

'But...that's just it! The fact that we haven't, that's what makes it so perfect. No explanations, no pretense, no pressure of appealing to each other. It's a holiday we both take from our everyday lives.'

'His intentions are questionable. You can't deny that.'

'Piya, he's a near thirty-year-old overenthusiastic lad, a bright one at that. Who the fuck cares about his intentions?'

'Just keep your antenna up, that's it. Meanwhile, you're doing good, woman. It is pouring men! Amen!'

'You make me sound so hormonal!'

'Amaya Kapoor, you're single, footloose and fancy-free. It would be okay to be a horny bitch too.'

Eight

Born and brought up in Delhi, Zahira Siddiqi moved to Mumbai in her early twenties to pursue a career in advertising. Along the way, she fell in love with the camera and that affair has outlasted all others. Today, she is a well-known professional in the world of photography and photojournalism. She divides her time between Delhi, her real home, and Mumbai, her foster home, as she likes to call the two metropolises.

Intriguing insights into 'Delhi-men' and 'Mumbai-men', in areas of attitude, mindset, and intellect are documented in this delightful coffee-table book. Interspersed with parallels and observations through photographs and quotes, the differences reflect in language, dialect, predilection and sensibility. In the crossover section, 'converts' like her—men born in one city and now living in the other—find a place.

Zahira Siddiqi and Amaya Books give you *Male of Two Cities*.

'How's that for the blurb?' Amaya asked Zahira after reading it aloud.

'It's too wordy! Overwritten. Makes me sound like a flower.'
'It's all yours to edit and deflower then.'

Amaya buzzed her dad's office.

'Dad, Zahira's here. Do you want to join us for a bit?'

Hanging up, Amaya continued, 'He's so excited about this. In fact, he's fascinated that such a fancy could be turned into a book.'

This book had Anand Kapoor all perked up and he was often involved in the brainstorming sessions. The father-daughter duo was thoroughly enjoying the workspace.

'We have to give it to him, Amaya. His inputs are priceless. It's a pity he didn't lend himself to be featured as one of my subjects.'

Anand Kapoor walked in just then. 'So, what do you think, Zahira?'

With a gleam in his eyes, he pointed towards the final proof of the cover.

'I think that you're a rockstar, Anand.'

'Aah, now that's a terminology I can still understand. You never know these days. The dumbing down of language is heartbreaking. What's that word that kid used the other day, Amaya? The one who came in with her first draft?'

'Douchebag?'

'Yes! Why would someone complicate a term as easy as "idiot" to call it that? Anyway, now what's next? Have you two zeroed down on the choices for the two launches? I want this to go as per schedule, Amaya. You have two months.'

'We're working on it, Dad. The crossovers are finalised. I think Gaurav Sharma is a unanimous choice. He's agreed to do both the events. The rest should be sorted by next month.'

'I still can't believe we've pulled this off! It started with an indulgence and now it's a piece of work, literally,' Zahira said.

They flipped through the final proof. It had seemed quite far-fetched at a conceptual level; but once Zahira had juxtaposed it into a narrative, Amaya was completely sold on the idea and had a great time putting it all together. Amaya also knew that since the book was so 'today', there was huge scope to devise winning marketing strategies for it. They had planned two back-to-back launches in Delhi and Mumbai. An interesting list of people was being shortlisted to make the sessions engaging. The journey of the two women in the making of this book had been a rewarding one and they intended to keep it that way.

Raina was finally ready to talk. Amaya had never been one to crowd people's personal spaces. And an 'I told you so' never did any good to anyone. She was glad Raina called her and Amaya immediately agreed to meet up, hoping that it would be an opportunity for her to fit in the missing pieces of the puzzle.

During lunch, trying to zero-in on a venue, Amaya audaciously texted Virat.

'Hey, how's it going? Planning to swing by GREEKY for a drink and a quick bite. You around?'

Virat's instantly replied.

'Finally! You've taken up my offer. Sure, I'll be around.'

Deciding that there should be full disclosure, she said she was meeting up with a friend but would drop in a bit early and see him.

'And for a moment I thought this was all happening for the love you had for me!'

She chose not to reply to the text and left it at that. She called Raina, who was hesitant to go back to the very restaurant where she had embarrassed herself. 'Amaya, I made such an ass of myself there!'

'All the more reason to go there! It would do you good to be seen as the person you are.'

'But what if Virat is around?'

'He will be, and that should be fine. You've got to take things head on, face your demons, Raina. Isn't that the plan?'

She reassured her that nothing could go more wrong than it already had. Raina eventually came around. Amaya walked into GREEKY, asked for Virat and settled herself on a bar stool. He was with her within minutes and glided to give her a peck on the cheek.

'Hey there, gorgeous!'

He held on to her a tad longer and tighter like he usually did when they met. Then, he asked as she released herself, 'What's your drink?' She opted for a Hoegaarden draught, her current favourite, and after signalling the bartender for two beers, Virat added, 'You know your beers well, unlike most women.'

'That's sexist!'

'Okay! Okay!' He raised his arms in defence. 'So how much time do we have before your date arrives?'

'My "date" is Raina, and let me warn you, she's extremely embarrassed after what happened that night. So, you'd do good to not bring it up.'

'Aah! Not to worry. I'm not so gauche. And to think about it, she gave us a good review in *Notebook Delhi*, so I owe her one anyway.' Giving Amaya a top-to-toe look-see, he said, 'You're getting hotter by the day, sweetheart.'

'You aren't doing badly yourself.'

'Oh well, I don't need to try too hard,' he shrugged smugly. He really didn't. But he also needn't make it so glaring. The man was so full of himself. Maybe he ate ego waffles for breakfast!

'So how is the place doing?' Amaya asked.

'Keeping me busy. It is picking up and all of us are putting in extra hours. But I do get lucky sometimes when a pretty lady decides to give me company,' Virat said with a wink.

'On that count, you must be a very fortunate man.'

'That night was something,' he said, looking right at her. She should have known. Virat wouldn't miss an opportunity to bring that up. 'The night' had been something.

'I'll say it was,' she added, keeping with the tone.

'Hmmm, being so close to you...Amaya, I was so turned on! You seemed pretty into it, too. '

'Yeah, I'm like that once in a while.'

'In that case, I need to be around you more often, who's to know when the mood strikes again.'

'Don't count on it. You should know, since men never miss an opportunity to take a dig at women and their, as you call them, "mood swings"!'

Before the innuendo-heavy conversation could go any further, Amaya spotted Raina walk in and gestured her over.

She hugged Amaya and looked at Virat. 'Virat, that awkward moment, huh? I'm braving huge embarrassment by just being here today and standing in your presence. That would be a good enough reason to be excused for my conduct the other day. My bad, really.'

'Hey, it's cool. Consider it forgotten. By the way, thanks for the write-up.' He then added, 'Try the cocktails. They are refreshing innovations and have been specially created by an internationally renowned bartender! You girls have a fun evening.'

Amaya gave Raina some time before she unravelled the story about her marriage and the aftermath of its failure.

'I couldn't place a finger on it at first. Obviously the first conclusion was that he was cheating on me. The signs were all there, but so was the denial mode. But never in my wildest dreams did I imagine it to be another man. It's weird, a part of me was relieved that it wasn't another woman; somehow that hurt less. At least my self-esteem didn't take a hit. But that was just the tip of the iceberg. Soon, it became even more obvious that it wasn't just one man; there were many men. Once he realized that I knew, he became open about it.'

'The world's full of schmucks!' said Amaya.

'He played on my sympathy and how. The hackneyed tale of being confused about his sexuality, how he had really tried, the it-wasn't-me-it-was-him story.'

'So, you became the proverbial victim, huh? Succumbing to drugs, alcohol, sex? That's the predictable story too, isn't it?'

If Raina was hoping to get pity from Amaya, she'd have to look somewhere else.

'I took refuge in whatever came my way. It began as a craving. I'd crave food and alcohol and then OD on both. I never became dependant on alcohol. I just used it as a means to an end. What I started needing the most was sex. Maybe just to get back at the man I got married to, or to feel more wanted; I don't know. What started as a carnal need became an obsession. At first, it was with a couple of guys at work; it was fun, quite crazy and comical at times. I mean I'd just proposition one of them and voila! Life was good. But then it became rampant. I'd walk into a bar and just want to be gratified with any man I found desirable. When I couldn't get it, I would get wild, and then obviously, the pills would follow.'

'The ones you found desirable. Thankfully, some quality control there, eh?' Amaya said.

'Yeah, you could say that now. Some standards were maintained.' Raina let out a relieved laugh at Amaya's attempt to lighten the mood.

'Well, if sexual healing's what you're looking for, then, babe, you are in the right city. That much I can promise you and it's okay as long as you're careful. Just don't mix it up with the meds!'

'That evening was insane. I chased the pill with vodka after the longest time. Guess it was the euphoria of meeting you and believing nothing had changed.'

'Well, you almost did pick up the doctor at the hospital!'

'Amaya, I am so, so sorry.'

'Hey, it's over now. Behind us. Especially for you. By the way, I have the number of the doc from that night, in case you wanna go for him. Else there is Mr Bakshi here with his overactive libido.'

Raina scoffed, 'Yeah, but he's married!'

'Oh, that's hardly an impediment for him; or for that matter, for many. Just a heads-up though—Virat Bakshi is an emotionless player. If you want him, play this his way.'

'I think I need to go off men for a while!'

'There is a lot more to you, Raina. You're a smart, intelligent and gutsy woman. You're nobody's fool. All this that has been a part of your life, don't make it your life.'

'Yeah, I am moving in the right direction. My folks have been so supportive, though they don't know too much about my issues. I'm piecing my life back together and I'll get by with a little help from my friends.' She squeezed Amaya's hand in gratitude.

'Amen to that!' They moved on to talking about work and other bits to fill each other up on their respective lives. It had been a good evening and the more they talked about Virat, the more Amaya was convinced that he would make the perfect prototype for the Delhi launch of *Male of Two Cities*. The mental note of floating the idea by him and thus watch him gloat was made.

The two women chit-chatted a little while longer. The evening strengthened their existing bond. The years they hadn't been in touch seemed to just melt away. On her part, Amaya was happy that she had helped unburden Raina.

Amaya clearly remembered the night that had been the topic of conversation with Virat. How could she not? It was etched in her memory.

Soon after the launch of GREEKY, Amaya and Virat had met again at a regular Delhi party—a clone of many others—at a new nightclub that claimed to have taken the city by storm. Delhi's hotspots, like in most cities, were short-lived in their status and each enjoyed the limelight till the next one superseded its popularity. Her first thought on entering it had been that she was getting on in years, as she had immediately wanted softer music and brighter lights.

David Guetta's beats had the dimly-lit floor going manic; Amaya had been tripping on the track, swaying her body and feet. Before she knew it, Virat had come next to her. He had further closed in on her. She remembered feeling his heavy and inebriated body as she had rested her hands on his shoulders. In the next instant, his hand had slid up her back under her loose chiffon top. Responding to the touch, Amaya had instinctually tightened her hold on his shoulders. Taking the cue, Virat had started caressing her skin slowly. It had been a mad, sensual moment, with Virat's body almost touching and teasing hers, her breasts pressing closer to his chest.

The two of them had moved completely in sync and Amaya had been consumed in the moment. She hadn't realized how long that spell had lasted but she had hoped that it would remain between them. She couldn't have been further from the truth. Both Virat and she had been oblivious to the fact that there had been one person who had witnessed it all. Without any remorse or guilt, Virat had texted her the following morning.

'You looked stunning last night…impossible to resist…'

'Careful now, Virat, not being able to resist oneself can prove hazardous.'

'With health hazards like you around, poor men like me hardly have a choice.'

'Poor man, my ass. A man like you is spoilt for choices.'

'There are plenty of fish in the sea, but who cares…'

'Yeah, it's all about the one that gets caught in the bait, eh?'

'Nah, that's easy. It's more about the one that escapes. That's the one I have my eyes on…'

Amaya was always a little lost when it came to Virat. His reputation preceded him by leaps and bounds. He was a man who was used to getting any woman he wanted. And did he want a lot of them! Whether Rupali was oblivious to his escapades, or chose to be, was anybody's guess. And at the cost of being immodest, Amaya knew that she was at the top on his list of pursuits. She knew this was one chase Virat would be willing to put his money on. She could hardly blame him. Her giving in to the moment, even for a flash that fateful night, had obviously fuelled his desire.

Remembering the happenings of the night, she didn't realize when she drifted into sleep. She was awoken by a phone beep. It was a few minutes past one in the morning. It was Rohan.

'Teacher, got a minute?'

'What are you seeking?'

'The word "calling". What does it mean to you?'

'Purpose of life.'

'Bingo! You found yours yet?'

'Uh…no! Why do you ask?'

'Just.'

'Have you? Btw, beer doesn't qualify.'

'Funny. I'm in the moment, babe…'

'Aren't you always? Just, till the next moment comes along.'

'Okay. Focus now. You haven't found your calling. So, what's the plan?'

What plan? I'm not going to globe-trot looking for it. It will find me if it has to!'

'And if it doesn't?'

'I won't be surprised.'

'Huh?'

'This new-age mantra of finding one's calling, what gives? What if I don't? What if I don't *want* to? What if life passes me by without that moment? If we keep waiting, we might just spend the better part of our lives doing just that.'

'Point being?'

'That we should do good; do what we know best. And spare ourselves the agony involved in the pursuit of this "calling" business.'

'But that's where the "calling" intervenes, doesn't it? To tell us what we're best at.'

'That's valid. But our definitions of "best" are exclusive to us. My "best" right this moment is indulging someone to figure out his calling; making this moment worth his while. He may not find it, but I tried. Don't let the moments pass you by, Rohan. The trick is to tweak the narrative.'

'I think I just found it. You.'

'Nah! But maybe, just maybe, you're getting closer to tweaking the narrative.'

'It's insane! Why did I come calling out to you at this hour? Why do you have all the answers I need?'

'I don't. But as always, happy to help!'

'Happier to be helped!'

'Where are you?'

Amaya's query was left unattended as that was the last she heard from him that night. It was just so 'Rohan' of him to evaporate out of a moment, just like that.

Nine

$\mathcal{A}$maya was at the site of the bookstore. She gazed at the walls that were covered with beige-coloured sundried bricks placed horizontally. Wooden bookshelves were tucked away comfortably in some areas and suspended in the others. The backs of the shelves were devoid of wood so that the walls could be visible with the books resting against them. She intended to make the space appear more like an elegant living-room area than an overcrowded bookshop with customers unable to find the books of their choice.

Amaya worked with the interior designers to create the same effect in the main area. She, along with the design team had selected couches upholstered in earthy solid colours. Recliners would cover two corners of the floor space. It all seemed to be coming together slowly. It was just a matter of time when the most talked about bookstore would be open to Delhi.

She returned to her office to oversee a couple of covers and run through a new manuscript she had found promising. But she wanted to take more time to decide. She asked her assistant to fix a meeting with the author for the following Monday. Amaya liked to work on deadlines as that way, she was confident of getting her work done well and on time. Her mind went to the first-time authors whose lives at that point depended on a 'yes' or a 'no' from her. She felt their pain and as a policy, she ensured that she got back to them in a month with her decision. That was non-negotiable.

Her sporadic Scrabble sessions with Rohan were getting more intense. It was something Amaya had never experienced before—she would look forward to getting back on the board with him, not so much for the game, but more so for their chats. She realized that it was an excuse to get to hear from him, given his propensity to come and go without notice.

'What brings you back on the board?'

'My pursuit of enlightenment! Lady, please impart the pearl of wisdom for the day.'

'Word of the day: Sapiosexual (n): one who finds intelligence the most attractive sexual feature.'

'That's a cool discovery. They actually have a word for it?'

'Seems like it.'

'So, are you "sapiosexual"?'

'Well, as they say, intelligence is the ultimate aphrodisiac.'

'Got to agree on that one. Wise minds think alike!'

'And…differ too.'

'But that's what makes talking to you a mental exercise by itself. One can never catch you off guard. Do you ever give your mind a rest though? Or is it always in thinking mode?'

'It mostly is. I'm just not wired to go off it.'

'Give it a rest lady…do it for me. Sapiosexuality aside, that blessed mind of yours needs a holiday! Give this one a think, will ya?'

Ten

Amaya gave herself one final look before heading out. A black woolen polo neck and flared knee-length skirt, a Hermes stole thrown on her shoulder, a comfy pair of heeled boots, hair left open, a pair of hoops and a watch—the only accessories—was the dress code, as laid down by Piya.

It was a long drive from her place to Noida. She had been there a few times, but was still somewhat unfamiliar with the area. It seemed like a labyrinth to her on every visit. She instructed her driver and then sat back, listening to her favourite band Coldplay's music.

Looking out of the window, her mind went back to Amaya Books and More. She was making a few mental notes when her phone beeped. A text from Rohan via Facebook Messenger. It seemed silly to her that they hadn't exchanged phone numbers, as they weren't strangers anymore. She felt that she knew him and he understood her better than many others who were privy to her cell phone details. She decided she would soon change this minor technicality.

'Hey Retro...'

'Hey there, wise guy, how goes it?'

'In Bangalore...at a bar after an honest day's work.'

'A drink well-deserved then. What could be better than a chilled beer?'

'You got it, lady. That's the plan. Give a tired guy some company? That is, if you aren't busy.'

'Never too busy. How's the weather at the bar?'

'Waiting for it to get hot!'

'Yeah, you sound like you've been cool for a while. Hot would help.'

'How'd you guess that? You a mind reader?

'When a young hot male is at a bar after a day of hard work, it doesn't take much to figure what he wants next. How long in Bangalore?'

'I leave tomorrow.'

'Then step on it, boy. Your time starts now!'

'I am not robotic. I have to get the feel.'

'Oh, don't worry about the feel. That comes as and when the weather gets hotter.'

'I think it just did! Catch you later, babe, gotta go...'

Tarun's directions were spot on and soon Amaya was at his rooftop bachelor pad. He led her across the chic living room, towards the balcony where a handful of guests were warming themselves around a bonfire. She didn't display her surprise, but none seemed to be writers; at least none that she could place. The home was very 'un-writer' kind, as she would later tell Piya. Pieces of straight-line, contemporary furniture were placed immaculately. Dim lights and green plants accented the charming terrace. Amaya soon found herself chatting with her neighbour at the makeshift bar.

'There's something about Delhi winters, isn't it?' he said,

taking in the cold air and digging his hands deep into his jeans.

'Sure is. It's great to be in a city where seasons change. It would be so drab to be in the same kind of weather throughout the year,' she added.

'Yeah, gives us so much more to look forward to.'

'Totally. Makes us more versatile as people, eh?'

'Hmmm, not too sure on that one. We're a pretty stuck-up city!'

'Who was it that said that conversation about the weather is the last refuge of the unimaginative?' Tarun joined them, handing Amaya her drink.

'Not when we're talking about Delhi winters. That stuff lights up the eyes of many a Dilliwaala!' Amaya said.

'Beautiful eyes, might I add then?' Tarun added.

Tarun introduced Amaya to the other guests. It was an interesting lot that included a tabla player, an adman, a young pretty girl who confessed she was still finding her calling, another extremely attractive website designer, and a dancer.

'And this is Amaya, the lady responsible for my nomadic scrawls finding a resting place,' Tarun said, while introducing her to his guests.

'That's a rather embellished introduction!' Amaya said, a tad bit embarrassed. 'Tarun's scrawls, as he calls them, would have become what they are, with or without me.'

'Okay, that's as much mutual admiration as we lesser mortals can handle!' said Malini, the dancer.

'I agree.'

The conversation carried on.

'What dance, Malini?' Amaya asked her.

'Kathak, now merged to become Sufi Kathak.'

'Hmmm! That sounds really cool! Tell me more,' Amaya said.

'Can't really be explained. Are you familiar with Kathak?'

'Somewhat. I trained for five years as a kid but gave it up eventually.'

'Okay. So, we combine the basic moves of the dance with Sufi music and ideology.'

'So how many public performances do you give annually?'

'Delhi is mostly restricted to the winter months. So, during the summers, we try and pack in as many national and international performances as we can. In fact, we performed in Boston in September. And before that, at the Smithsonian in Washington. I must say, the crowd comprised more foreigners than Indians.'

'That sounds really great! What could be better than making a living out of one's passion? This does seem like something I'd love to know more about.'

'Why don't you come by our studio? See what we do.'

'Sounds good.'

The two women exchanged numbers with Amaya promising to be in touch soon.

'I'm happy to see you are feeling comfortable among strangers,' Tarun was soon by her side.

'Oh, meeting new people doesn't faze me. In fact, there is something brazen and enriching about walking into a space full of unknown faces. I find myself taking away a lot more from them than I would from a gathering of friends, acquaintances and adversaries.'

'That's because you're a peoples' person. For us introverts, such spaces can be daunting. But you, Amaya, are compelling company for me. Am I glad I mustered the courage to invite you here tonight!'

'Why in heaven's name did he require "courage" to extend a casual invite to her?' she thought to herself. He seemed intimidated by her; that seemed odd to her as not once during their meetings had she gotten the impression that he lacked self-confidence. On the contrary, vainglory had seemed to be his stronghold. In between all this, her mind kept wandering to Rohan. She kept checking her phone to see if there was a message from him.

'I can't keep my eyes off you, Amaya. And you can't seem to keep yours off your phone.'

'Are you flirting with me, Tarun Bhaskar?' Amaya asked him, amused. She hadn't realized her actions were so noticeable.

'I'm really not great at this so-called flirting thing. But if that's what it takes to get your attention, so be it.'

'You already have it, Tarun.'

'I'm a writer, Amaya. My wooing skills are a bit jaded.'

'Well, then you should know that I don't need to be "wooed". And I don't need the disclaimers.'

'That is a relief. I like your straightforwardness.'

'Never thought of being any other way. Though yes, I am a little surprised that "wooing" me is a part of your plan.'

'Been on the agenda for a while. I just needed the right moment.'

A beep on her phone threw her off the conversation. It was from Rohan.

'Sorry! It's got smokin' hot in here and I have her company.'

'No worries. I can disappear anytime you want.'

'No, don't. I'll be back with you soon.'

'There're better things to multitask at! Shift your focus to the one by your side.'

'She's there all right. Hoping she gets closer!'

'What more could you ask for?'

Assuming that he had found his date for the night, Amaya concluded that she wouldn't hear from Rohan for the rest of the night. She threw her phone in her purse and decided to have a pleasant evening. And pleasant it was, with light conversation, drinks and hot, barbequed snacks. It was refreshing, Amaya thought to herself, to once in a while encounter people from various spheres rather than always be surrounded by writers.

Amaya had ample time to think about the conversation that had transpired with Tarun on the drive back home. He hadn't wasted much time in making it obvious to her that he wanted to take their professional relationship further. But his behaviour and comments had sounded cheesy and so contradictory to the articulate vocabulary used in his writing. No, she did not have 'beautiful eyes'! Her eyes were small, almond-shaped and nobody had ever called them that.

It was the age of 'instant gratification', and the principle could be applied to all layers of life. These were the times they lived in—the times of Facebook, Instagram, et al—where the 'like' and other emoticon keys were punched sooner than later. On that note, she gave Tarun a 'like'.

Amaya's curiosity got the better of her the next morning, and on her way to work, she texted Rohan.

'Guessing the temperature did go up last night.'

'Yeah! The beers added to the foreplay and the rest…well, is history, as they say.'

'History, already? Give the poor girl a chance!'

'She had her chance!'

'What a player!'

'Me? A player? Nah…I just know how much potential there is to things…'

'You don't even give it a chance! Is that the right way?'

'Works the other way round, wise one. Chances are given on the basis of the potential seen.'

'Yeah, then again, maybe she didn't see that potential in you either.'

'Huh?'

'Maybe she was the player and she played you.'

'Huh?'

'It's not always about Mr Right. At times, it's only about Mr Right Now.'

'I never saw it that way…'

'You're welcome! And something tells me you aren't too pleased with the revelation.'

'I've had them better. This one got me. And something tells me you've played it well, coach.'

'I've had my moments.'

'So, how was your evening?'

'Good! With potential, too.'

'Aah! I like the sound of this. Matching up to your standards is a tough game. Good to know someone has the making.'

Rohan. He flattered the woman in her; he indulged her condescension. It worked every time. If he was playing the game, as was Piya's intuition, he had his strategy worked out. Or maybe, he was just made that way. Whatever it was, she was enjoying her exchanges with Rohan and strangely, she missed them when he was silent.

Eleven

It was a busy day at Amaya Books, and Amaya was all set for the back-to-back meetings for the launch of Zahira's book, *Male of Two Cities*. Everything about the book—from the cover to the content—was explosive. Not in the controversial sense, but one that would make people sit up and actually take notice. It was a piece of work that all those who had lived or were living in either of the cities, could relate to. If there was one thing Amaya Kapoor had understood in the last ten years of being in publishing was the fact that not all books were about receiving awards. Some were fillers between the bigger and glorious moments. Yet, they remained for long on bookshelves and in the hearts and minds of readers.

Zahira was almost convinced on having an all-women group release and discussion of the book, whereas Amaya felt that for a more lucrative sales and marketing pitch, it would make more sense to have a representation of both men and women.

'It'll be too bland, Zahira, with just women holding the stage. They'll turn it into a feminist-sexist gig.'

'But why would that happen? Let's get their take on a book full of men. We'll keep the crusader lot out of it.'

'I still feel that we should get the men in; they can be so bitchy. The two teams can bandy about and keep it alive. Don't you agree?'

'Yeah well, you're right about men being bitches here. Let's try and find some who make the cut and then we can take a final decision.'

They spent the next two hours brainstorming over the names. Amaya was keen on Virat Bakshi as she felt he was the most representative of the archetypal Delhi male. That guy epitomised the 'male of one city' and how! He was so self-obsessed, in all probability, he wouldn't be able to crack the subtle pun. Of the six women they zeroed in on, they would select three, and two male celebrities featured in the book. After giving a few suggestions and unanimously agreeing on Gaurav Sharma as one, Amaya left the Mumbai lot in Zahira's hands giving her carte blanche to go with the team she wanted. They decided to meet again in a week's time and finalise the list once and for all.

Amaya's team was excited about the new book as they knew that once again they had a bestseller in their hands. Bookshops all over the country were clamouring to get their advance stocks and most had promised to give the book a special display that had been put together by Amaya's marketing team. Leading bookstores in both Delhi and Mumbai—as the book centred on the two cities—had affirmed to put up hoardings at prominent places and pitch in with advertising. It would be showtime soon!

Amaya was looking forward to her date night with Tarun; it had been a while since she had gone for one of those. Even before she could fathom a reason for her eagerness, she was punching a text to Rohan.

'Got a date tonight!'

'About time. And who is the lucky one?'

'A writer friend…'

'Aha!'

'His new book is going to be a bestseller, btw.'

'You would know, that's why you're publishing it.'

'It's a brilliant read. Totally sold on it.'

'And on him, eh?'

'Not quite, but I'm working on it. Hoping tonight will be a starter…'

'Hell, I hope it's a main course and dessert as well! Add a nightcap to it too! Where are you guys meeting up?'

'Olive.'

'Nice. A favourite of mine.'

'Mine too!'

'What you wearing?'

'You my date supervisor or what?'

'Why not? I'm making sure you give the guy what he wants. It takes one to know one. I'd say, you're going with a pair of jeans and a hot black top. Less fuss, more flair.'

'I must say, your study on me is progressing well. Soon, you'd have achieved a Master's.'

'Long way to go, and I have my own modus operandi on how to get there. Inshallah, some day! But for now, you have a nice eve. Look good, feel better and be the best!'

'Thank you! You have plans tonight?'

'Yup…planning as we speak! Later, then.'

A chat with him was always a riot. And easy! He was non-judgemental, concerned just the right amount, and not overly curious. It was good to have him in her life, not that without him, she had been missing much. But with him around, she was getting a bonus she had never thought she needed.

She gave instructions to the household staff as she had been doing for the past week since her folks were travelling. As she was getting dressed, she laughed to herself as she recalled Rohan's advisory.

Jeans, fitted black sweater top, high heels, kohl-laden eyes and a light lipstick with her hair falling straight—pretty much the basic look. Amaya was good to go. She would meet Tarun at the restaurant; he had offered to drop her back home. She reached the restaurant, tucked away near Qutab Minar. The outdoor seating was inviting during the winter months with a crisp nip in the air. Tarun was waiting for her when she walked in. Clad in jeans, a white T-shirt and a casual navy blue jacket, she noticed that he was dressed differently from his usual look.

'You look ravishing,' Tarun said, greeting her.

She thanked him and they ordered their drinks—vodka for Amaya and red wine for Tarun.

'Thank you for accepting my invite.'

'Oh, come on. You needn't be so formal. So, tell me, how does it feel to be on the verge of a new book?' Amaya said, deftly changing the topic.

'Calming! I've done my job. The rest will follow,' he said self-assuredly. They chatted about many things, including the new writers in the scene. They discovered that they both had a passion for travelling.

'If only one could spend one's life in travel mode, seeing and soaking in the sights,' said Amaya.

'Yeah, living by the "life is a journey" metaphor, quite literally.'

'San Francisco,' pat said Amaya when he asked her about her favourite city. 'It's got the perfect balance of creative, contemporary, liberal and scenic. I could go back there any number of times. What about you?'

'I'm not a huge fan of the American dream and the country's non-existent culture. For me, it's Prague.'

'Oh! That was sharp. Prague is on my wish list too. Is that why Adil is based in Prague?' Amaya asked, referring to the protagonist of his book. 'Is Adil you? Semi-autobiographical?'

'Well, I like to actualise a bit of my own self in my creative expressions. It is the one familiarity I can rely on while weaving stories with imagination.'

'Eloquent, indeed! No wonder people love to read you. This one's going to be a sellout, Tarun, and I'm going to be one happy woman.'

'I'm certain there are other ways too, to make you a happy woman.'

'There's a whole list!'

'You really are something, Amaya. And the effect you have on me is far more intoxicating than this wine.'

There goes the eloquence! Amaya thought to herself. Coquettishness had never been her forte. After two more rounds of drinks and a sumptuous meal, they left the restaurant and got into Tarun's car. Amaya could sense a vibe between them during the drive back home and when Tarun pulled up in front of her house, she invited him in for a nightcap with her thoughts involuntarily deflecting to Rohan's allusion of the same.

'C'mon in. Let's see how serious you were on your bid to

make me a happy woman.' She was a bit high and well, it had been some time since she'd hooked up. Tarun was a willing partner and once in the house, Amaya led him straight to her room.

They started making out almost as soon as he was next to her on the bed. He ran his hands over her back and hesitated for a second before he nuzzled her breasts. During all this, he kept cooing her name every now and then. It was distracting; she liked lovemaking to be silent and intense. Tarun's cheesy liners continued to punctuate his moves as they undressed each other. 'I've wanted you since the day I met you...' he said, sounding besotted. She tried to ignore his words, she was driven. She needed him and that's what mattered. She played submissive, letting him move the way he wanted to. He did and she responded. She climaxed before him. And then they both did it again.

After it was over, he was lying next to her, heaving with satisfaction. Amaya lay quiet, rested on the inside and the outside. Tarun turned to her side and cooed in her ear, 'You have me spellbound, Amaya...'

Spellbound! Another one! She couldn't indulge more schmaltzy declarations made by him. If only his words would emulate his writing. She smiled back at him, 'Tarun, stop paying me these tributes.'

'It will be an uphill task, but I'll try...only because you want me to.'

The ardent admiration was freaking her out and she hoped he'd leave before she said anything uncomplimentary.

'I hope I gave you all you wanted and I promise to compensate next time for wherever I was lacking.'

Compensate! Lacking! What was it with him? She wanted to scream but held herself back. All she could come up with was,

'Don't be so hard on yourself, Tarun.' He gave her a sheepish smile, and was soon off.

Okay, so that had turned out different than she had fancied. Tarun's words had always allured her. But it was one thing to be in awe of what one perceived of a person and another to then see the same person with his sheen stripped off. Sex with the writer may have satisfied her immediate urge, but it had been a little too less to evoke a desire for more. Maybe she could attribute it to the fact that it was the first time with Tarun. There was a possibility it would be better the next time, but she was quite certain there wouldn't be one. Shaking away her thoughts, she wrapped herself up in the duvet and checked her phone, only to see that there was a text from Rohan about an hour ago.

'R'ber what I said…nightcap!'

Amaya messaged back.

'Yes, night-capped!'

She immediately realized the idiocy of her actions. She had barely finished having sex with one man and was texting the other! Her phone buzzed with his reply.

'Nicely done?'

'Don't know about nicely, but done…yes!'

'Ooooh! Don't tell me the prolific writer couldn't perform as eloquently!'

'No comments.'

'Yep! Some things ARE better left unsaid. Have always told you that you're a tough one to please.'

'What are you doing up so late?'

'I've got a life too, albeit not as active as yours! I was just about to turn in, but a text from you is irresistible at any hour.'

Rohan had shown no surprise or amusement at her candid texting. He had taken it as a given. It was bizarre how unabashedly they were willing to confide in one another and accept each other's confessions.

Twelve

$\mathcal{A}$maya was going through the provisory menu of the café. Some stuff looked good while she was dissatisfied with the other suggestions. She was deep in thought when her phone beeped. The message was from Rohan.

'Hey Retro, what's up?'

'Usual work stuff. What's up with you?'

'Ditto! Waiting to get out and down a few beers. Watching the match!'

'Okay…'

She typed, her mind still on the menu, making a mental note to check on the pastry chef Piya had recommended.

'You seem pensive…'

'Do I? Sorry, just in the middle of something…how come you're off work at noon?'

'Low day. Need to recharge. Lack of alcohol stops my thinking process, you see. What's on your mind though, coz there always is something, lady.'

'Not a good idea to tell someone who's not thinking till he's drinking.'

'Hold that thought. Keep it on "to be contd." mode. Packing up at
work. Catch you in a bit.'

Amaya got back to sorting out the menu, making calls and
confirming the sampling of desserts. While conceiving Amaya
Books and More she had decided that she would have four
distinct menus—one each for the four seasons of Delhi—spring,
summer, autumn and winter. Along with the ample choices of
books and other creative activities, she wanted the food to, in
a sense, complement the bookstore. Around two hours later,
she received another message from Rohan.

'Cheers! My thinking cap's on.'

'Now we're talking. My utmost gratitude to the beer, for giving a man
a halo on his head.'

'The Dutch are grateful and wanna reciprocate with a kiss... Muah!'

'The Dutch?'

She then realized he was referring to the makers of the beer.

'And who might the Dutch be to give you such authority? Do women
never have any rights?'

'They do but they seldom refuse a guy with a halo over his head!'

'Some might....not all of us are that hot on angels!'

'Blasé, eh?! Not pushing this one as I certainly don't intend to market
myself. You've made your choice.'

Uh-oh! There she'd gone again, sounding supercilious. 'Not
so hot on angels'—aargh! But he'd put her in her place.

'I'm already sold on you.'

She added in a bid to undo her uppity remarks.

'Hmm…that's better! You Dilliwallahs…diplomacy is your middle name.'

'Don't OD on the thinking though, your halo might just fall off!'

'I'd be okay with that, since some of you aren't that "hot on angels".'

'We are flirty today, aren't we?'

'That is indeed a thought! A little flirty might just be the flavour of the day, if you do so oblige.'

'Oh well, why not?! A little flirty didn't hurt no one.'

'So…you aren't hot on angels, eh? What gets you hot then?'

'You really want to know? Haven't we talked enough about this before?'

'Uh-huh, not even close to enough. With you, there really is no saying. So, go on…I'm all eyes.'

'Well, a working mind would be one to get me started!'

'Okay, so that one's covered. What else?'

'And here, we women are accused of vanity.'

'What else?'

'Sense of humour, decent looks, dependability….and I'm guessing you've got that covered too!'

'Bingo! Must say…hasn't taken you that long to figure me out.'

'Huh? Last I knew, you were the one trying to "figure" me out…pun totally intended!'

'Whoa! You are a bright spark! See, this is why it's

always stimulating to make conversation with you.'

'There we go again! I'm thirty-five going on forty, not a wide-eyed, eager-for-praise babe. We could do without the flattery.'

'Why is it so difficult for you to accept a compliment gracefully?'

'Why is it so difficult for you to understand that "compliments" don't do it for me?'

'I'm not trying to do it for you! I meant what I said if only you would take me seriously!'

'If only you would be serious, would I take you seriously!'

'I am serious. I mean it.'

'Copy that. Hey...I'm sorry...'

'Don't need to be...it's cool. Go easy on me, Amaya. I'm not trying to get anywhere you don't want me to be, so relax! And I'm not going to justify this anymore...'

'Noted!'

The singles' gang left Kamani Auditorium where they had all gotten together to watch a play. Much before the newer theatres came up, Kamani was *the* place for anything and everything Delhi wanted to watch live. Amaya was glad that she had got this break as she knew she was in for a hectic time with the upcoming two-city launch of Zahira's book. The gang then headed to the Gymkhana Club, where Thursday nights were very 'happening'. In the heart of Lutyens' Delhi, the club attracted people of all ages. The young mingled pleasantly with the elderly, chatting over a drink and even dancing to a live band. There were several regulars at the club, and even if one forgot a name once in a while, there was the 'Gymkhana' familiarity and camaraderie. Amaya herself had been a regular here since her college days.

Amaya had seamlessly drawn Raina into the group and she fit in perfectly. They were hanging around at the crammed island bar. The tables were already taken and the bar too was overflowing. The group was talking about the play and Mihir was all praises for the female lead, a known theatre and film actor.

'She's dusky and sensuous!'

'Did you catch the nuances of the play or were you just ogling Meera?' Noor quipped, referring to the character enacted by Mihir's current muse.

'Babe, I lust only for you,' Mihir mouthed a remark to appease Noor.

The play had been centred around the theme of modern marriage and a young, urbane couple's challenge to keep it going. With the two actors as the voice-overs, it questioned the sanctimony of the institution. The subject wasn't new, but the way it had been approached had made its mark. What Amaya found impressive was that it showed the wife coveting and desiring another man's affections. In the context of the English theatre scene in India, this was an avant-garde move.

'It can drive you crazy to be with just one person. To think she's known only one man sexually!' Noor said.

'But that's the case more often than not, Noor. It's almost as good or bad as being a virgin!'

'Monogamy is so overrated. Got to hand it to the play though; it's pretty daring to openly voice a woman's sexual desires. I'm glad such things are finally finding takers,' Raina said.

'I'm sure that the thought has crossed the minds of many, but we're hard-wired to live in denial under the garb of right and wrong,' Amaya said in agreement.

'Yeah,' Noor carried on, in unison. 'I mean, much of this is dated. Take premarital sex, it is so last season.'

'Wonder why it's called "premarital" anymore, considering one may not ever get married,' Amaya had them cracking up.

Raina was about to say something but thought better of it and let it go. Later when Noor was out of earshot, she told Amaya she had assumed Noor and Mihir were a couple.

'They are what is nowadays termed as "friends with benefits",' Amaya updated her. Raina nodded.

The club was buzzing. Groups, large and small, were hovering around at the spacious bar. Members and guests paused to greet friends and familiar faces every now and then. The smokers were converged at the porch overlooking the sprawling lawn. Noor was in her element and was urging Mihir to take a few random shots. Amaya noticed how well Raina and Mihir seemed to be getting along. Raina was laughing out loud at something Mihir had said and had her hand on his shoulder. Well, as long as Noor was okay, it really wasn't her concern anyway. Being committed or not to one partner was a personal call and she wasn't getting into any tangles trying to untangle emotions.

She was missing Rohan. She was surprised at herself and how she was feeling; he was increasingly becoming a behind-the-scenes influence in her life. With so much Rohan on her mind, Amaya sent him a text.

'Hey…missing you!'

She was hoping to get a reply soon. She did get a message, but it was from Virat.

'Hey there hottie, how've you been?'

Well, Virat would get lucky that evening!

'Good. And you?'

'The same, *yaar*. Work and more work.'

Another text. It was Rohan's response to her text.

'You are? Where are you?'

'Out…with friends.'

'You're out partying and I'm being missed? And being texted! This, I like!'

'Yeah…I have been thinking of you.'

A parallel buzz from Virat.

'You there?'

Back to Virat.

'Yup! I am.'

'You seem busy.'

'Nah…just a bit of this and that.'

'You've been on my mind.'

'Have I? And I thought you said you were in work mode?'

'I am, but when I think of play, you are an inviting thought! And right now, that's what I'm thinking of.'

She deftly handled the arithmetic between human chatter and texting. Rohan's text next read.

'Prove it then.'

'Huh?'

She punched back to him.

'I'm so goddamn sure you're looking like a pic I'd wanna see.'

'Hmm...I'm in the mood to oblige!'

'Hmmm...bring it on then... Show me what you got, Retro!'

'Hold that thought.'

Amaya asked Noor to let her take a peek at the shots taken. 'Here, this...it's the best one.'

'Yeah, this one will do,' and just as she had tapped the 'send' icon, she realized she had sent the message to Virat instead of Rohan!

Fuck.

She had just obliged the very willing Virat with a very provocative picture. He would read so much more into that. Amaya looked around helplessly for Noor who had stepped out for a smoke. Fuck again! This had got to be *the* tech-un-savviest move of the decade! As expected but not desired, without much scope for damage control, she got an instant beep from Virat.

'Whoa! I didn't expect to get invited this soon!'

She was so miffed at herself. And just then, Rohan texted back.

'Ain't that a bit too long for a guy to hold on to his thought?'

'Well, what do you know, Rohan!' she thought.

It would take her forever to get into an explanation so she sent the same photo to him.

'Sexy! Sexier cleavage...if I may add.'

'Trust you to come up with something like that.'

'Trust me! Not all décolletages look good. And these days, you can never tell if what shows on the outside is the real thing. Damn the inventor of push-up bras!'

'Agree. Push-up bras are an optical illusion!'

'Another wise one from the wisest of 'em all. So...as always, with you, one gets what one sees, eh?'

'Don't know about "gets" but it sure is what one sees. And now if we're done with discussing my boobs, I need to get back to the radius I was in before you distracted me.'

'Yeah...I have enough thoughts to "hold" now! Thank you for the pic, lady. I'm stoked!'

He signed off, his last retort a perfect mix of naughty and nice.

Staring at her from the inbox was another rejoinder from Virat. He had returned the favour by sending his own bare-chested picture. Oh! Good heavens. She neither had the energy nor the inclination to go on any more with the pseudology. She returned her full attention to her friends and socializing with several other people, many of whom she hadn't seen in quite a while.

Thirteen

*D*amn the flu! Amaya surfaced post noon. She'd been under the weather the past three days, feeling drugged with the horrid medication; a real bummer of a weekend. Having nursed the flu enough and finally banishing the pills and syrups, she made a quick call at work and got an update on the goings-on. Checking her messages next, she saw a text from Virat. It was from last night and referring to the party she had missed.

'Why aren't you here? Was hoping to see you...'

She replied.

'A bit under the weather.'

'Would a kiss help?'

'Not really... '

'You're one of the few that make those unbearable evenings worth looking forward to...get well soon, and meet me sooner.'

What had begun as fun and games was getting her all bothered now. Why was she entertaining these overtures from Virat anyway? Would she have to make herself accountable because of that one 'off' moment where she had lost control? A woman like her should know better than to succumb to his ways and inconsequential flirting, which was his wont with anyone with breasts.

Feeling a shade better later in the evening, she lazed around the house with her folks. It was a nice cozy night. Her mom, dad and her were doing their own thing and yet being together over easy conversations, television and food. She had a couple of glasses of wine but they hit her faster than usual, and she realized it was because of the medication. Amaya sent a text to Rohan who had been missing in action again. She hadn't heard from him on the board for the past ten days.

'What is it with you? You have a fetish for going incommunicado!'

An hour went by before she heard back.

'That's just the way it is with me, babe, you know it. If you wanna associate with me, you gotta deal with it.'

'Wanna *associate*? Mighty snobby that!'

'Lighten up! What's with the crankiness? You've been missing me, eh?'

'Where have you been?'

'Work! Work! And work!'

'You make it sound like you're the only one that works!'

'Nope. But I'm the only one that works the way I do.'

'Yeah, and for those mortals whose lives depend on associating with you, that's part of the package deal, huh?'

'Hey! I know you've been missing me. Now stop being a drama queen.'

'Care to tell me what's been going on with you?'

'Working my butt off on clinching the mother of all deals. But it's good to hear from you, as always. Another thing, don't take my disappearing acts personally.'

'How is that possible? Dude, that neon "DO NOT DISTURB" sign is in ON mode!'

'There is no DND sign for you and you know it.'

'Tough to look past it when it's blinding you in the eye. I can't have this one-sided communication going! Sorry, but that's not my way.'

'Your way. Let's talk a little more about that.'

'There you go again.'

'I've had a rough day, sweetheart. Gimme a smile and tell me what's been happening with you.'

'Rough day? What's up?'

'Don't wanna talk about it and you don't wanna read about it. Let's hear more about you.'

'Well, let's see. Being hit on by a married chap, a new book on the block, crankiness due to a man playing truant...that should sum it up!'

'Someone's been busy! Btw, I am not surprised about the pass made on you. You're irresistible.'

'Et tu? I'm not in a mood for any more patronizing, please!'

'Hey...wanna go for a drive?'

'Huh?'

'Great weather here. Let's do the drive. Consider it a date.'

'My first virtual date!'

'I am all yours for the rest of the night. You deserve the indulgence after your action-packed week!'

'Days without a word from you and this "back with a bang" style of yours is too much to handle. I can't do this switch-on-switch-off…'

'My bad. My work takes me away, but I'd like no one else but you to bring me back…'

'You know, all these things you say…'

'I mean every word. It's you who always overthinks everything. Could you just let go for a bit, please?'

'Oh! What the hell! Let's do this!'

'That's my girl! You're the best! Cheers!'

'Ain't I? So, what are we toasting to?'

'To us!'

'There's an "us"?'

'Hell YES! To you and me who are now in a space called "us"!'

'I like that—"in a space called us". We've come a long way, from strangers to friends to "us".'

'Uh-huh, Amaya Kapoor…now I'm not going to let you Q&A me on "this space called us". Take that thinking cap off right now.'

'Done.'

She did just as he asked, still holding on to his words.

'I'm going to be in Mumbai on the third for a book launch. You're invited if you aren't too busy. Check your mail for details.'

'Sure thing! Finally, you in Mumbai on my time!'

'I'll be flying out the next morning. Staying at JW Marriot. How about you buy me dinner after the event?'

'Just dinner? No vodka for the soul?'

'That too! Don't stand me up like you do virtually.'

'Not a chance! Waited for this for a LONG time!'

They chatted till the wee hours, he in his space, she, in hers, and 'us' being a rather ambiguous zone. She hadn't felt so intimate with someone in a long time.

Fourteen

The Mumbai launch of *Male of Two Cities* was all set to take place at the iconic Prithvi Theatre in suburban Juhu. It was a personal favourite of both Amaya and Zahira. A family legacy, it had an intimate theatre space, open-air café—a chilled-out hangout for theatre lovers. It was a place where one was bound to bump into a celebrity or more, casually enjoying the famous Irish coffee et al, after a performance. Prithvi had an indoor amphitheatre, and the idea was to have Zahira and the gang right at the centre, surrounded by the audience.

Amaya had discussed all the details with her father and he was rather pleased to hear their plans. He chose to stay back in Delhi to oversee the preparation of the launch that was to be held the very next day, after Mumbai. For Mumbai, Siddharth Mehra, a forty-year-old actor, activist, model and thoroughbred Mumbaikar had confirmed his presence. The official release would be followed by an interactive session along with the author and six other participants that included—Aryan Dutta, the young bohemian actor; Sanya Kumar, an upcoming star-daughter who was an avid reader and hence associated with most book events; Gaurav Sharma, the young talented director working with a top film banner, amongst others.

Gaurav was an interesting pick since he was a convert. Having lived in Delhi throughout school and college, he moved to Mumbai and had been there ever since. His first directorial venture was based in Delhi, and he featured in the book too. The others included the heir to a big business empire, Azeem Kothawala; a prominent hairstylist and an ambassador of Gay Pride, Rhea Rao; and Shaheen Baig, a forty-year-old columnist and novelist.

The cover design of the book was the Mars symbol entwined with graphic maps of Delhi and Mumbai and characteristic slang words and expressions picked up from local and English lingo printed in the background, with black, white and lime green being the only three colours used.

On her way to the hotel in Mumbai, Amaya texted Rohan. She was completely focused on the event, but getting Rohan into the picture had her sidetracked, albeit momentarily. She was all butterflies! Meeting the man who had become a part of her life demanded the excitement.

'Landed!'

'Welcome to my city! Hey, did you say the launch was at five?'

He sounded like his usual self, caught up at work.

'Yes, at Prithvi.'

'Hmm…sorry, hon! Don't think I'll be able to make it to the event. God knows I so wanna, but duty calls. How about we meet straight at the restaurant? Sending you details…'

'So long as you're there! Don't wanna be stood up.'

'Don't you worry. I will be waiting for you. Want me to carry a red rose or something so you can spot me easy?'

'Nah…'

'See you very soon then.'

The release was an orbit of hyperactivity from the moment the panel was showcased. Amaya was, as always, the generous publisher, letting Zahira take over the limelight. Sid Mehra helmed the launch with glitz and glamour. Gaurav Sharma was at his witty best. He read from the book and drew interesting parallels on the men that were covered in the book. The women provided friendly banter by taking on the men. The Dilliwallahs versus Mumbaikars debate was a riot and the intelligentsia indulged in lighthearted tête-à-tête.

It was a wrap. The panel moved off the platform and chatted with everyone present. Amaya spent the next hour with the panelists and guests. She could see the look of contentment on Zahira's face. Copies of the book were changing hands and drawing the attention of the crowd. The publisher's job was done. Amaya moved off the arena with a quiet yet sanguine move.

Not wanting to miss a single minute with Rohan, she took off and headed to the popular beachside restaurant, one she'd heard a lot about. On reaching, her eyes were searching all around and she finally spotted the face that bore resemblance to the pictures encrusted in her memory.

He rose from the chair with a look of recognition and stood with his hands in his pockets as she approached him. He was dressed neatly in a navy A&F T-shirt that showed off his fit body and a pair of jeans.

'Rohan?' she asked. He bowed his head slightly and moved his hand forward. She grasped it and gave him a hug—her first effort to break the ice, if there was any. His cologne and body scent hit more than just her olfactory senses. It was heady.

'You look good. Black seems to become you,' he complimented her on the knee-length loose black outfit. 'Shall we?'

As he moved to pull the chair for her to be seated, Amaya said, 'Let me take a good look at you.'

'Ha ha ha! Amaya, just the Amaya I have been chatting with.'

'Why would you expect anyone different?'

'True that!'

She could sense him sizing her up and her 'vital statistics', but he did so with panache.

Once seated across him, Amaya tried to superimpose the real image of the man with the one she'd visualized in her mind time and again. The person before her was a six-foot tall man, with a deep throaty voice, large intense eyes, aquiline nose, extremely kissable lips and a five o' clock shadow that was just right. The stubble made him look mature. She couldn't wait for Piya's reaction. It would probably be 'babe, he's too good to be true' and she'd have to agree. Rohan Kashyap looked better than she had thought he would.

'It doesn't seem like I'm meeting you for the first time,' Amaya said with a relaxed smile.

'Yeah, it feels like a movie where we've reincarnated and this meeting brings to mind some vague memory from the previous birth, eh?' he winked. 'By the way, your looks totally defy your age. You should stop calling yourself old, Retro, seriously!'

'And you look far more mature than I had imagined you to be.'

'I've been working on that ever since I encountered you! Got to look less like a lad.'

'It's working.'

After ordering a round of drinks and a salad and starter on his recommendation, they started talking as long-lost friends did, bringing up bits of the chats they had spent hours on. There was so much they still didn't know about each other—the customary 'favourites', birth dates, the familial story, the people they admired, the ones they didn't think much of, books read, places visited. Rohan told her he was an only child; his dad headed an MNC and his mom was a high school geography teacher. He had moved to a place of his own four years ago, just to make his life easier and spend less on the Mumbai roads since his workplace was in suburban Andheri and his folks were towners. He then asked Amaya about her familiarity with the city and she told him she'd visited Mumbai a few times.

'For work?'

'And pleasure. Mumbai is a city where you always find people you know…'

Rohan was showering her with attention and there was nothing to complain about. She was all-aglow in the flow. He asked her about her bookstore and Amaya's eyes lit up as she gave him a detailed lowdown on it. She wanted to know more about him and his life and so she asked, 'Your work is your passion, isn't it?'

'As I can see, so is yours. But to answer your question, yeah, it totally is. Nothing else can keep me going. I've wasted many years on irrelevant things, getting absorbed in the wrong priorities. Besides, it's a new company, there's so much to be done, so much to be achieved. I can't afford to lose my focus anymore.'

'Wrong priorities? There is something I don't know, isn't there?'

He smiled and changed the topic, 'Too much to do, too little time!'

'And miles to go before you sleep?'

'Very much so. You're no different! Work's your driving force too, isn't it?'

'It is, but not in an obsessive way. Most of us are so passionate about life's components that include work, marriage, kids, love, sex, duty, et al. But I live a life, not just work. I want to put in that extra mile to keep the balance going. To make sure the components are in balance, and when not, push hard to restore the equilibrium. I don't want any more "blink and you miss" moments in my life, Rohan.'

'I envy you. You make it sound as if it is all within reach, like it's a walkover. For me, it's just my work as of now. Of course, I do more, at least it seems so, but nothing would count if I can't take my working day forward.'

'That's the road you've taken. You keep moving forward single-mindedly, taking breaks with the people and moments you encounter en route your destination. Me, I don't want to take any one road. It has to be a series of alleys, flyovers, bridges, and skylines. I want to be able to dart across from one space to another just because I need to be there or maybe, because I'm needed there.' She paused, completely submerged in her rumination. After a few moments, she looked at him and said, 'Much as I like to fly, sometimes, I'm quite content being the wind beneath the wings.'

'A complete and sorted demarcation of your passions. Like I always say, you are my path to enlightenment, lady. And a gorgeous one at that. So, tell me, Amaya Books must keep you very busy. How do you make time for other stuff, especially the board?'

'It's my timeout, my extended world of words.'

'Don't you have to deal with enough words already?'

'Is there such a thing as "enough words"? What can I say? I'm a self-confessed logophile.'

'A what? Slow down. I am a mere mortal. Logophile?'

She laughed and said, 'A lover of words. That's a logophile.'

'You know you should hold vocabulary management sessions.'

'Words fascinate me. Their sheer power, what they can do or undo, is intriguing. I can never tire of them. And there is always a new word on the block.'

'You fascinate me!' he retorted with utmost honesty. 'I've never met any woman who said that.'

'You're only thirty! They'll be many more.'

'How does that matter? There still will be only one warped Amaya Kapoor!' came the skewed compliment that she knew was so typical of him. 'That bookshop you plan to open...you should do this "word of the day" thing there.'

'Nah. It's pretty commonplace now.'

'Look at the canvas of words in you. You should take it upon yourself to contribute to the vocab education of your city.'

'True that! But I'm not convinced.'

'Nothing new there. You do drive a hard bargain.'

Amaya looked at her watch. 'Should we call it a night?' she asked somewhat reluctantly. There wasn't any other place she'd rather be than with him.

'Don't go just yet. Stay. May I remind you that you owe me some "thinkless" time? Come with me, just a few more hours and I'll drop you back safely to your hotel.'

'Come with you? Where?'

'Trust me, it's nowhere you wouldn't wanna be.'

What did he have in mind?

'I trust you, but if that "safely back to the room" doesn't happen, then you are so fucked.'

'I'm aiming to get there even before!'

'You wish!'

Amaya knew it was crazy to go along with him. She should have been heading back to the hotel to get a good night's sleep. But spending a few more hours with Rohan was a thought too tempting to let go.

Just then, his phone rang. 'Hey Guy, will be there in twenty and Amaya is with me.'

'Where are we going?' she asked him. It was all happening too fast for her to process.

'You'll see in a bit.' He disconnected the phone, turned to her and said, 'Not to worry. You're safe with me in my city.'

Soon, they were at the door of a seventh-floor flat of a suburban high-rise building. As they walked in, a gorgeous young girl greeted them. She gave Rohan an affectionate hug while Amaya stood by. A minute or two of discomfort was put to ease the moment she was introduced to Gayatri.

'So, you are *the* Amaya!' Gayatri aka 'Guy' said.

Amaya gave Rohan a quizzical look. He shrugged in defence.

'Yes, that would be me!' she said.

'Yeah, she is the one and only!' Rohan added, grabbing a copy of *Male of Two Cities* from Amaya and handing it to Guy. She took a good look at the cover and added, 'Hmmm...interesting. People, look what I got here,' she signalled to some of the guests around her as she walked past them towards the bar.

'This copy's sure gone in the right hands. Let's hope it stays in one piece before the night ends!' Rohan said, watching the book passed around.

'As long as it does the rounds!' added Amaya.

'So, Guy and I are school friends, have known each other for the longest time. She's Ms Bollywood herself. She's an AD with Rajbir Singh Productions and is one of the most ambitious women I know. Watch out for her!'

Amaya took in all the information.

As they moved in the crowd, Amaya was greeted by a lineup of enthusiastic and exuberant people from different walks of life—some were Gayatri's 'filmy' lot; some Rohan and her friends from school and college, while others were partners of the friends. Soon, it became apparent to her that Mr Rohan Kashyap was quite a star there.

It was a balmy evening. It hadn't taken her too long to feel a part of the crowd, even though they were all strangers. She had been welcomed by the host and the guests as if she was one of their own. She realized this was, to her, a notable difference between Delhi and Mumbai. The former took its time to warm up to new faces.

Rohan was by Amaya's side most of the time, yet not overly fussing, leaving room for her to get acquainted with those she chose to. She did catch him and Gayatri engaged in an intimate conversation while she was entertained by a young, 'high', aspiring director, who gave her an account of the highs and lows of the film world. There was an immense flow of energy all around.

'Hey babe, you doing okay?' Gayatri came up to her.

'Yes, thanks! You have a nice place,' Amaya engaged her in a bit of polite conversation and it was only a matter of time before they started chatting about Rohan.

'He's a workaholic. Ever since he launched his new company, he's been unstoppable!' said Gayatri.

'Yeah! His work gets his adrenaline going!'

'Funny you should say that...he says it too, all the time! You have quite an impact on him.'

'Oh, you know your pal well enough, he loves the drama!'

'True that!'

She saw that the man in question was keenly watching the two of them, but opted to not participate in the conversation. The two got on to talking about each other's professions.

'You run a publishing house. That's something,' Gayatri said to Amaya.

'And you make movies.'

'It's what I've always wanted to do.' Gayatri's determination impressed Amaya. It was no surprise that Rohan and Gayatri were friends.

'Tell me more about your glamorous world,' Amaya asked Guy, genuinely interested in what she did and how that world operated.

'It seems more glamorous than it actually is. At our level, it's as much blood, sweat and tears as in any other profession. The actors are all real people with the same issues like anyone else and that's how we deal with them.'

'Hmm. By the way, I believe your head honcho, Rajbir Singh, is planning to write a book. That would be some book to publish.'

'And you call us workaholics. Look at you!' She gave Amaya a look of admiration. 'Yeah, that story seems to be doing the rounds. In fact, I think we had some Delhi publisher come by the other day.'

Amaya's antennae were up. 'Oh! Who?' She asked, trying to sound casual.

'I don't know the details but I can find out for you,' Guy said.

'That would be great. Amaya Books too would love to bid for the project.'

'Will do! And whenever I direct my own film, maybe Amaya Books will publish a book on its making. What say?'

'Fantastic idea! For some reason, Amaya Books has strayed clear of anything filmy. But I'm open to it.'

Amaya made a mental note to dig deeper into the possibility of making Rajbir's book happen. One book like that would lead to the kind of publicity that ten books would garner. And the genre excited her—Indian filmmakers were making a massive impact internationally as well and Rajbir's autobiography would instantly mean an international edition.

It was way past midnight and the guests were all drenched in smoke, alcohol, and more. Amaya had been occupied with endless conversations. In need of solitude, she wandered out to the balcony that overlooked the beach. The heady combination of vodka, the breeze and the sound of the sea was blending perfectly with her mood. She leaned against the wall, soaking in the moment.

'It's stunning, isn't it?' Rohan said, standing close to her. He gently tucked a few strands of her windblown hair behind her ear.

'That it is, undoubtedly. This is something we Delhiites don't have. It's so mesmerising, I can be here all night long...'

Rohan didn't fumble nor was he unsure. He held her face close to his and kissed her passionately. She was powerless. Her arms wrapped around him as she responded feverishly to his mouth. She felt the wetness as his tongue moved in and around her ear. His hands were stroking her back and she held him at the nape of his neck. The rush was undeniable. Amaya rested her head on his chest.

He stroked her hair and they caressed each other. He then pushed her aggressively against the wall, moved his body forward and kissed her again—deeper and stronger.

'I'm so drunk!' Amaya said.

'And I'm high on you.'

His desire was obvious.

'I told you, leave that mind behind and I'll take you places.'

'Rohan...'

She wanted more of him. She pulled him and he kissed her again, moving towards her cleavage. She was completely oblivious to her surroundings. All she could feel was Rohan. He looked at her in a way that said it all. Suddenly, Amaya stepped back into real time and looked at her watch.

'We better get going. It's close to two in the morning and I have to be at the airport by eight! I'm sorry.'

He snapped. 'Sorry? Why'd you have to say that?'

'Just...'

He took Amaya firmly by her hand. After saying goodbye to everyone, he helped her into his car. She must have dozed off for a bit because Rohan gently woke her up outside the hotel.

'I better escort you to your room.'

'Yeah...I'd like that please.'

In the elevator, they kissed again and then, once again outside her room. She was resting her head on his shoulder; her hands were on his lower back, not wanting to let go. He pulled himself away, opened the door for her and said, 'You better get inside.'

They looked deep into each other's eyes. She wanted him to come in. She wanted more of him. But her mind took over her heart and body. It would be too soon. She wasn't prepared, she was not 'there yet' for Rohan to make love to her. But... but...she was prepared! It was all she wanted. Could it be the alcohol and the abandon that was making her feel this way? She could see the desire in his eyes, too. And she was sure he could see it in hers. As if on cue, Rohan kissed her on her forehead and said, 'Goodnight Amaya!'

He took the decision for the both of them and it probably was the right one. They hugged and he left as she shut the door. She leaned back on the door, breathing heavily. She came right that instant and that proved to her that maybe, just maybe, she should have allowed him into the room.

Back in Delhi, she was still heady about the previous night, the only clarity in her head being her desire for Rohan. Why had she not invited him in and why had he not insisted even once? Neither of them had lost control and maybe that was the sad part. One move by him and she would've have not stopped at the door. Maybe one by her would've led to the night playing out differently.

The Delhi event was scheduled for five in the evening. That gave Amaya enough time to take a power nap. Delhi worked well, the big clincher being the book's reference to the capital's affluenza syndrome—the city's obsession with one's address and all other things being a derivative of it. 'Where do you live?' was the typical conversation opener of the city, and its reply determined whether the asker deemed it 'influential' enough to take the conversation any further. Thus, ensued a debate about how the identities of Delhites remained attached to their domiciles, occupations, the cars they drove and how opinions were formed and judgements were passed based on them. Zahira was as upbeat as she had been in Mumbai. Virat Bakshi delivered well and was surely the right choice for the position of one of the panelists. Gaurav Sharma recounted the difference he had observed being 'a male of two cities', bringing forward a contrast in the attitudinal elements of Delhi and Mumbai.

'Virat, you were superb. Thanks so much for this,' Amaya said to Virat.

'Hey, it was easy. I just had to be myself. And you're going to have to find a better way to thank me. How about you buy me a drink and express your gratitude?'

All this while, Amaya was under the illusion that getting Virat on the esteemed panel would suffice as gratitude. He should have been the one thanking her.

'Sure thing,' Amaya left it at that, as she had no intention to spend an evening with Virat. It was shaky ground to be with him and would be best avoided.

She waited till night, resisting every urge to connect with

Rohan. Luckily for her, she had a busy day to keep her mind off him.

But she finally relented.

'Thank you for a fabulous evening, and more so, for acting like a responsible adult and sticking to my Cinderella time.'

'Your affect is contagious, Retro. I find myself "maturing" in your company. It was a perfect evening. Just perfect. Conversation, laughter, alcohol, music, and the rest was a bonus! Btw, you *are* a good kisser. Such a bummer you had to leave.'

'You should be glad! Too much of me isn't a good thing.'

'"Too much of you" has me scheming already. From the sample I got, I can't wait to discover more. The next time we meet…you're my date.'

'Date! Ahem!'

'Yeah! It should be obvious now that I would officially like to move out of the "friend zone", as you call it.'

'You would now, eh? And what is the zone you'd like to move into?'

'I do have a few in mind.'

'Smart move!'

'You haven't seen any yet, lady.'

'I saw some last night that left me wanting for more.'

'The lady flirteth! I must have done something right!'

'That's the thing, you did everything right.'

'Hmmm. And that gets you thinking, doesn't it? You can never stop the overthink, can you? It's in your DNA.'

'You know I'm wired that way.'

'If it makes you feel any better, I was just being myself which is easy
to do with you. Don't worry your pretty little head;
we got a good thing going.'

He was right. Their meeting had been an extension of
the 'text'ual relationship they had shared so far. Rohan's sheer
physicality, the energy of his presence had her enthralled. His
combination of boyishness and maturity was lethal. Their
chemistry had been electric. Amaya couldn't wait to get more
of him. She smiled at the serendipity life had offered her. After
a long time, she had met a man who had her smitten.

Fifteen

*P*lanning ahead for the next two weeks of her absence, Amaya delegated work to her staff that she knew was well-trained to handle even a crisis situation. The next consignment of the furniture for the bookstore would arrive after her return. The rest, her dad was around to handle.

Back home at five, she had three hours to wrap up her packing. The much-awaited trip was finally here. Two weeks with her sister and brother-in-law, away from the madding crowd. Amaya was closest to Anahita in the whole wide world. She missed having her around. If there was one thing she wished for, it was that she could be with her more often. But, this being another imperfection of her life, she was thankful that they were in the Internet age, where distance got negated with a video or audio call.

On the way to the airport, she and her mom chatted about the exciting holiday ahead. Neena was glad that Amaya was getting this well-deserved break and her two daughters would get some quality time together. Amaya hugged her mom tightly and bid goodbye. After going through immigration and security, she waited for boarding in the business class lounge. Sipping on red wine, she thought of sending a message to Rohan. As was typical of him, he had gone off the radar and there hadn't been any communication between them off late. Amaya was getting used to his missing-in-action mode, but it did leave her baffled. Invariably, it was always her who resumed contact after the gaps. At times, she wondered if he was at all interested in being in touch with her, if at all he had meant all that he had said, and the biggest, if at all had their steamy rendezvous left as much of an aftereffect on him as it had on her.

Letting out a sigh, she texted.

'California East Bay Calling! Two weeks of timeout.'

Amaya got an instant response.

'Is that an on-text or off-text two weeks?'

'That would depend on you. I'm not the one who goes in the off-mode.'

'Hey, c'mon! How many times do I have to tell you to not take that personally?'

'Hear! Hear! Easy for you to say! Anyway, boarding now...later.'

'Fly safe, babe, have a blast, keep it fun. Try not to "think" too much.'

'I'll try. We know how tough that can be!'

At the airport, the two sisters united in a super hug, as if to compensate for the time spent apart. It didn't take long for the 'Anahita mode', as the family called it, to kick in.

'So, you have tomorrow to rest and get into the groove for the rest of the blast you're going to have here. Friday is First Friday, which you just have to do! Weekends are usually on Nikhil mode and pace, you know how he likes to "chill" on his "two special days". Monday through Wednesday is your "me-time" with Berkeley and books. Come Thursday, it's both of us on a roll,' Anahita said with a big fat smile and twinkling eyes. Amaya knew it was pointless to ask her to slow down.

Her darling sister thrived on living every moment—'killing it', as she always said. And that was exactly what Amaya needed.

Anahita had never confined herself to her father's or sister's space. She had drifted out of the 'lit-zone', armed herself with a B.Com degree from Shri Ram College of Commerce in Delhi and moved to San Francisco to pursue a career in accounts. She would visit home every year but was certain that a permanent move to India was out of the question as she loved her life in California. She had met Nikhil five years ago and they had been married for three.

Amaya was so proud of her baby sister, who was now working in a high-powered Fortune-500 multinational accountancy firm. She worked long hours but loved every minute of it. The couple had recently shifted to Oakland from the South Bay area—a bigger place—in anticipation and preparation of a baby. Anahita called it the 'nesting' phase. Nikhil too had an enviable CV. With an engineering degree followed by an MBA from an Ivy League, he was working with a leading computing firm.

The two sisters, five years apart, bore a slight resemblance. Anahita, standing at 5 feet 7, carried her wavy hair a tad shorter than Amaya. Both had an almost identical physique, with the younger sibling always borrowing clothes from her 'di' or elder sister's wardrobe during their growing years, till of course the jeans, trousers and skirts started to wear short on her.

Amaya told Anahita that her first stop had to be to a network service provider. Staying connected was her lifeline; she was comfortable with the thought that anybody could reach her at anytime from anywhere. On switching on her phone, she saw a message from Rohan. He seemed to have kept the flight duration in mind and the text had landed probably the same time she did.

'Hey Retro, hope you had a safe flight and U. Sam welcomed you warmly.'

'Hey, thanks! Yup, flight was great...and the welcome couldn't have been warmer. Talk soon.'

'Let me guess. Rohan, huh? Man! Does he love you or what!' asked Anahita.

'He has me guessing that one,' Amaya said, feeling elated at the receipt of the text, yet not quite sure what to make of it.

Anahita and Nikhil were very proud of their house. The short driveway led to a porch and the first thing one saw was the beautiful handcrafted door that Anahita had gotten shipped out all the way from Jodhpur in Rajasthan. The ground floor had a guest room and study done up brightly in shades of blue and brown and scattered bits of green that almost made it seem like an extension of the impeccably manicured garden. Back inside, a small winding staircase with a wooden railing led to the master bedroom and another guest room that would be Amaya's.

She adored the four-poster bed with crisp white linen, pillows and cushions in one of her favourite colours—canary yellow. The house was warm, welcoming and it had just the right amount of artworks picked up personally by both Anahita and Nikhil on their travels around the world. Nikhil was home, waiting with a simple salad and grilled chicken meal ready for them. They caught up over a few glasses of red wine and the delish meal.

'Hey, I probably won't meet you all day tomorrow, so just to let you know, I've fixed up your Berkeley trip with Anirudh for Monday, as your sister is very keen you wrap up all your "literary agendas" by Wednesday,' Nikhil said to Amaya while planting a quick kiss on Anahita's lips.

Amaya had heard the name time and again over telephonic conversations to Oakland, when she had expressed her desire to visit Berkeley. Anirudh Kothari taught Public Policy at the Haas Business School at Berkeley, and was a close friend to both Anahita and Nikhil.

'Sure, Monday's good. Will he able to help me with bookstores and stuff, too?'

'He's all yours on Monday. Get whatever you can out of him' was Nikhil's hot lead to Amaya.

Sixteen

'Oakland First Fridays' was Amaya's inaugural experience of the event. The affair extended its arms to the city and its neighbouring areas on the first Fridays of every month. It started at five and courtesy this event, some streets in downtown Oakland's Telegraph Avenue transformed to welcome visitors from all across the Bay Area. It was touted as the premier arts event on the West Coast. 'It's like, every first Friday of the month, people get out on the streets to say "I Love You, Oakland,"' said Anahita who was a diehard follower.

Amaya was introduced to her company for the evening—Lisa and her boyfriend Brad, Nammy as in Namrata, Jay as in Jayesh, and Sally. These were familiar names from the conversations she'd had with her sister and she quite enjoyed associating the images in her head with their bearers.

Once in the arena of action, Amaya found herself in the midst of art galleries and artists, musicians, dancers, performers—bringing the streets to life. The gang strolled down the confines of this mega event, pausing at the eclectic spots of interest to absorb the adventure. Hip-hop, alternate rock and other new-age musical forms changed beats every few metres. Various art galleries were open to the public during these hours, some even offering free wine and nibbles. The streets were buzzing with masses of people thronging to enjoy the live music, street-food, local artisans and more. Amaya took to the goings-on of the ghetto-esque ambience with aplomb and let her hair down.

She sauntered into an art gallery that caught her attention. She got chatting with the young transgender artist whose works were being exhibited. One painting, in particular, drew Amaya's attention. It was contemporary and vibrant and a perfect piece to adorn a wall of the bookstore. Amaya bought the painting, convinced that for the holistic feel she wanted the store to have, the artwork was just right, especially since it didn't shout out loud a big or celebrated Indian artist's name.

They stopped every now and then at various drinking joints for beverages. A kiosk called 'Beeryland' caught her eye and she led the gang up there. No prizes for guessing the order that was placed. They were spoilt for choice with the list of beers on the menu. And since experimentation was the very theme of the evening, Amaya opted for a local brew. They all then headed towards a quadrangle that served an array of cuisines to choose from. Amaya spotted a streetcar selling 'deconstructed samosas'—that was enough to stir her curiosity. They discovered it was totally 'Oaklandised' with a mishmash of sauces, chickpea and fusion flavours. Nevertheless, it was delectable and savoured by all of them. The music was getting louder; the mood was getting lighter.

Anahita winked at Amaya, 'You up for a wilder time?'

'Why not?'

They stopped at a cart selling desserts. Amaya looked unsure, but her little sister reassured her, 'Di, it's just weed balls and you're used to that stuff.'

'Hell, it's been a while since I went down that road!'

'It's the same road, all been there, done that.'

And...why not? When abandon was beckoning she may as well go the whole hog. On that drift, she popped a small but potent, ball-shaped chocolate-covered sweet treat and soon, the out-of-practice Amaya was a milder but definite version of stoned.

As she walked down the street, zoned out, she thought of Rohan. He had wanted her to be in this mode, the 'thinkless' mode. What followed was a drunk 'typo-ed' text exchange which she had no virtual control over, literally. With the multiple intoxicants taking over, the rest of the night was a haze.

The next afternoon, Amaya was woken up with a big cup of coffee.

'Some night, huh?' Nikhil said.

'Thanks to your wife! Debauched night, might I add!'

'Well, at least you got the full taste of "First Friday",' he said laughingly.

Still hungover, Amaya could barely keep her eyes open and everything around seemed fuzzy. Taking a few sips of the coffee, she didn't realize when she handed the cup back to Anahita and snuggled back into bed. Finally surfacing later in the evening, having a vague memory of her textfest with Rohan, she went through the transcript of the chat.

'Here I lie…weeded and wasted!'

'Nicely done!'

'I WANT you here…I need you here, Rohan!'

'And I want proof.'

What had followed was evidence of her smashed state. Pictures of her looking high as a kite with a dopey smile, hair and sleeveless low-cut top, all awry, was what she had sent to Rohan.

'That's pure fireworks!'

'You…I can't get you off my mind.'

'Your mind…that's a fine place, though I can think of other places I'd
like to be in…'

'So can I…mmm…like my lips, my neck, my ears…like it was in Mumbai.'

'You keep on that weed, babe!'

'This is crazy…you and me….will it always be like this?'

'Will you stop thinking for once? Just stay in the moment. Let's get
back to the other places.'

'Soooo wish you were here. Lucky to have you in my life. You just let
me be ME…'

'But, that's the thing, you just are!'

'I know I just am…so stoned!'

'I'm loving it.'

'I must have done something right to have found you.'

'You haven't done much yet, but there are a few options you can
choose from.'

'Mwah!'

'Am taking the next flight out! This is too good to miss!'

'For real?'

'Woman, if I was there with you right now, this would get so real!'

'Be with me!'

'Your wish will be my command, soon…'

Anahita teased her. 'Those are some hot pictures you sent
him, Di.'

'Tell me about it. But that's not all. Look at the texts I've sent him!' She held her head in her hands.

Anahita was unfazed. 'What's the big deal? So, you were being affectionate, so what? Nothing crazy about that!'

'I was being bathetic and that is pathetic!'

She had sent three selfies to him in quick succession. That wasn't bothering her. The real reason for her angst was that he hadn't reciprocated with the same intensity. The man had kept it on the same level as always, being his flirtatious self. Some damage control was required, and that's exactly what she did.

'Mushy much!'

'Yeah, you can say that!'

'The side effects of substance abuse.'

'Must be that, to get to you this way.'

'And by this way, you mean…?'

'A tad too sentimental…'

'Hey…thanks! I stand warned now. You have issues with emotional paroxysms. Will keep a check on that.'

'Check on what?'

'The mush…I don't want to spook you. Anyway, there's nothing to worry about. Blame it on the weed and forget about it.'

'I'm not worried. That's why it is so easy being with you… You're way too smart to let sentimentality get the better of you.'

'True that! And that arms me with another weapon of Rohan-destruction. You get sentimentally-spooked.'

'I totally do. There, another side of my soul bared to you.'

A revelation, indeed! Rohan Kashyap, all of thirty, could effortlessly flirt with a thirty-five-year-old woman, feed her vanity, lust after her, deliberate over matters of her interest, but he could not handle emotions.

Amaya marvelled at his ease of compartmentalising life. So, 'sentimentality' stayed locked in a separate box, lust in another, worklife in the third, so on and so forth. He pulled out the suitable box at the right time, utilized what was in there, then packed it up and got the next one out. And in all this, that little box that had 'emotions' labelled on it, could lie languishing in an obscure corner of the mental loft, hoping that it might get its turn someday. People like him should have signed a 'pre-relationship agreement' that included a 'no sentimentality' clause.

She knew she was being a tad cynical. But it was good to know his side of the story. And if this was what he wanted, then this was what he would get. She'd be damned if she let him get the better of her in these mind games.

Seventeen

'So, I'm reconfirming with Anirudh for tomorrow. Let him show you around. It will be fun. He's a great guy,' Nikhil told Amaya.

Berkeley had been on Amaya's agenda from the very inception of this trip. She could use the company around the campus. She chose to ignore the thought that this could be an attempt at matchmaking by her sister and brother-in-law.

'He's a thoroughbred American, you know the "AB-not-so-CD" variety,' Anahita added, referring to the now commonly accepted acronym ABCD—'American Born Confused Desi'—used to distinguish Indians born in the United States, in contrast to those who were born overseas and later settled in the USA. 'And he's just what you want for all things bookish. The guy is a guzzler when it comes to reading.'

Anirudh and Amaya had an introductory tête-à-tête over the phone and fixed up a time to meet at Berkeley where he could show her around. He suggested that if they hit it off, they could probably 'do a coffee or a meal', depending on their comfort level. She liked his candour and told him she was looking forward to meeting him.

Later in the day, it was chat time with her folks. Amaya told her mom about the First Friday experience, tactfully omitting the 'culinary' details and then got on to a bit of work talk with her dad. He jokingly told her to ensure she did her homework on 'Mission ABM', knowing fully well that it was consuming her completely nowadays.

Wearing a basic navy-blue hoodie, jeans and comfortable walking shoes, Amaya was all set to encounter Associate Professor Kothari. She took the train to downtown Berkeley and relished the walk to the campus. Once there, she messaged Anirudh and in no time, she was hailed from behind.

'Amaya? Hey!'

'Hey! Wow! Had I not known it, I would've never guessed. You are a far cry from a professor at *the* Berkeley!' she said extending her hand.

It was true. He was reasonably tall, fair-complexioned, clean-shaven and sans the typical 'academic' air she was expecting. Neatly dressed in coordinated shirt-sweater and trousers, he said, trying to defend his community, 'We're new-age profs and like everything else new-age, we like to come differently packaged.'

'I better apologize for my lack of packaging then. I'm the good old brown paper bag and look every bit my part of a thirty-five-year-old Indian publisher.'

'Ready for a guided tour?'

He took her around, stopping every now and then, on either being beckoned by a student or colleague or at Amaya's behest for a look-see. The library fascinated her as most libraries did and she spent a considerable amount of time there. They decided to grab a quick sandwich and coffee at a café and music store, a stone's throw away from the campus and a favourite of the faculty.

'So, Public Policy, huh? It really can be quite a cracker of a subject to teach!' Amaya said, munching on her sandwich.

'I could say that to you. Publishing books…what more could a book-monger ask for?'

'Yeah, I think I lucked out on this one. It is a blessing, truly, to do what I love and love what I do!'

He asked her about the profile of Amaya Books. She gave him a brief lowdown saying that they were trade publishers and had a wide fiction and non-fiction list.

'So far so good, what say?' Anirudh asked her, looking for validation.

'Considering we're doing the coffee and the meal, that would be a yes.'

'I have been instructed by Nik to be your go-to guy during your trip. So, is there anything else on your list?' he asked.

'Well, since you're offering, I might as well grab all I can!' Anirudh broke out into an infectious laugh and Amaya noticed how his eyes laughed with him.

'What do you have in mind?'

'It's been a long day so I'll let you off the hook. But I would really like is to visit a couple of bookstores. Nik said you're an avid reader, so who better than you to take me on a bookstore tour.'

'Aah! Well yes, books and I do go together. A helluva lot.' He paused for a bit and then said, 'Wednesday is sort of easy. I'm done by four. So how about we meet here and I take you around? And maybe we could do dinner?'

'Perfect. I'll see you day after then, right here at four. Any changes, we talk?'

'Done.'

'Great! See you then.'

On Wednesday, they both met at the café and Anirudh suggested they walked to the bookstore that was just a few blocks away. The shop was visible from a distance, with its distinctive red-and-white awning. Once inside, Amaya felt like she always did in a bookstore—like Alice in Wonderland.

'I could spend my entire life in here,' she said to Anirudh. 'I'm gonna spend some time browsing, if you don't mind?'

'Go right ahead. I need to see some stuff too.'

Amaya moved from one level to the other, walking up the wooden staircase and stopping at the neatly arrayed shelves of books, keenly observing and selecting the ones she wanted to purchase. She also paid attention to the interiors of the store and started to note down the elements that could be used for ABM. The bookstore had a whole section of used books. She had never thought of that. ABM could buy used books and sell them at subsidized prices.

Ahead at a counter was placed tea, specially packaged for the store and available for sale; she sipped a spiced brew at the tea-tasting session, which she learnt was held at the store once every week. That was a good thought. The brand of tea she was planning to retail at the bookshop café, and even the green coffee, could be up for sampling. The possibilities were endless. There was a new idea afloat with every passing minute.

The collection of books was fascinating. From the latest to the rarified, they were all there; all that was needed was time and inclination. A big library chair or two were thrown around for buyers to rest and peruse the books they were keen to buy. What could be more aromatic than the smell of books? The whole experience was magical. Amaya spent nearly two hours looking around, taking notes, and making a final selection of the books she wanted to buy.

'I'm indebted to you for bringing me here,' she said to

Anirudh, who, too, seemed to have spent his time well, judging from the small pile of books in his shopping cart.

'Oh! You don't need to thank me. You could have done this by yourself. No big deal.'

'True as that might be, I didn't, and hence the gratitude to its well-deserving recipient. Dinner's on me, by the way.'

'We'll see about that. I've picked a place. How about some native Californian food?'

'There is such a thing? I thought it was all American!'

'Spoken like a typical tourist.'

They walked down two blocks to a restaurant that was considered to 'epitomize' what was popularly known as 'Californian cuisine.' Amaya curiously studied the menu. It was an upmarket place and as soon as they ordered a glass of wine, Amaya reiterated to Anirudh that dinner was on her.

'Ah! The passive-aggressive feminist,' Anirudh said half-laughing.

'Not at all', Amaya said.

The friendly banter continued over a sumptuous meal. They chatted about each other's lives; the comfort level had upped after the second meet. She quizzed him about his choice of profession.

'Two reasons: the first, I love to teach, and second and more importantly, I belong to the "slow movement" school of thought.'

Amaya recalled reading about this sometime back. The term had her intrigued enough to ask him more.

'Hmmm…tell me more.'

'It's about slowing down the speedometer of life. Inhaling longer and exhaling unhurriedly. A life far distant from fast travel, money, food, books, et al. Teaching gives me that.'

'Slow books? That's a thought,' asked Amaya, her radar

immediately connecting with ABM.

'Well, like all things else in the slow movement package, it's about qualitative and careful selection of the choice of books. In my opinion, it's reading good books against the trending ones. Spending time in bookstores as opposed to "click and buy" on the net. It's about feasting on your read.'

This information was priceless and she decided that it was a thought well worth mulling over.

'So, that's it. That's why I do what I do,' he said.

'Well then, Professor Kothari, might I add that you're doing it nicely! I'm all in for the slow movement camp.'

'And, your time starts now,' he said and Amaya went on to give him snippets about her 'life in Delhi'. She gave him a precise yet concise note purely on a need-to-know-basis. They both steered clear from personal details. She didn't ask him about his divorce that she had learnt about from Nik and he did not bring up any queries on her still-single status.

He asked her about her plans for the next few days. She said, 'What I definitely will be doing is visiting a couple more bookstores. That's for sure.'

'On the job even on a holiday, eh?'

'You can call it R&D. And since I'm certain you're a frequent habitué to many, please shed some light on the subject!'

He recommended a few bookstores in 'Frisco including the one that 'she just could not miss'—City Lights Bookstore on Columbus Avenue that had its roots in the Beat era. He felt it would be an immense experience.

'Thanks so much for the tip. I am just so excited and I know in my gut that I am going the right way,' she said.

They asked for the check and Amaya absolutely insisted on paying, but Anirudh did not allow her to do so.

'I may not be a CEO, but trust me, I do make enough

money to be able to take a lady out for a meal!' he said jokingly.

'And I'm not the passive-aggressive feminist trying to prove herself. It is just a small token of my appreciation,' she smiled back at him. He finally gave in. The drive back was so comfortable. Amaya felt content after spending a fruitful day and was much at peace in his company. Glancing at her phone, she saw a message from Rohan.

'How goes it, darl?'

Darl'? Well, well, a term of endearment indeed. She would never be able to figure this guy out.

'Boyfriend?' Anirudh asked, his voice not giving away his curiosity if there was any at all. Obviously, she had been engrossed on her phone and thoughts long enough for him to notice.

'Nah! Just a friend. Will deal with him later.'

Once home, Amaya thanked Anirudh wholeheartedly for the lovely day. She asked him to come in, but he declined, considering it was late.

'Do keep in touch. If you ever visit India, mark Delhi as a stopover.'

'I sure will. And thank you for the meal-you-didn't-need-to-pay-for, you know that.'

'But I wanted to! By the way you aren't the social network kind of person, are you?'

'You're right. That would be me.'

'I figured; it's too fast for the philosophy you believe in. We'll rely on emailing then.'

'You have a good time the rest of your stay. Anything else you need, call me maybe!'

The hug exchanged after that was warm and comfortable, the sort that signified they were welcome in each other's lives.

Eighteen

$\mathcal{A}$nahita was waiting for her and wanted to know every detail about Amaya's day. The siblings chatted over a cuppa as Amaya filled her in. She agreed that Anirudh made for good company and thanked her sister for connecting her to him. She had decided to wait till the next day before responding to Rohan's text.

> 'Hey, it's going super. Had an awesome day in the company of an erudite professor.'

> 'Nice! And what does she teach?'

> 'HE teaches business studies.'

She punched back, deriving devious pleasure from correcting the gender.

> 'Aah! So, someone's been up to something.'

> 'You could say that.'

> 'The sapiosexual in you getting aroused in esteemed company?'

> 'Well, a cerebral turn-on always works for me. Btw, you seem mighty curious about my extracurricular activities.'

> 'Don't worry. Just a harmless query.'

> 'Not worried! I'm just unable to put a finger on what your agenda might be.'

'Agenda? Where did that come from? Has thirty-five years of your presence on planet Earth not taught you that not everyone who crosses your path need to necessarily have an "agenda"? You disappoint me. For someone who distributes pearls of wisdom to all and sundry, you need a note to self.'

'Correction: I do NOT have a PDS of my wisdom!'

'Hell yes, you do. Life is good, woman, get one!'

'I *have* a life, thank you. What's wrong with you?'

'I don't walk into peoples' lives armed with an agenda. Believe me if you wanna, but I'm not wasting one more minute trying to convince you of "my intentions".'

She didn't respond. Amaya couldn't for the life of her figure out what she had said that was so offensive to get the usually unflappable and nonchalant Rohan to react in this manner. She'd let it pass. A twenty-nine-year old had to show his age sometime.

An hour later, there was more.

'Preparing notes for tomorrow's sermon?'

'There isn't going to be a sermon tomorrow...'

'Don't do this to me!'

'Where are you? What are you on? How many and counting?'

'How the fuck do you know I'm drinking?'

'You aren't just drinking, you are drunk!'

'I am, but don't worry. I'm too far away to do anything to you.'

'We'll talk later, Rohan.'

The exchange had irked her. It wasn't like Rohan to behave

that way. Later in the evening, relaxing at home, she wondered aloud his baffling demeanour. Anahita had her own theory. She was convinced that it had to do with Amaya spending time with Anirudh. Amaya rubbished that but the possibility meant that she had been able to evoke an emotion in the I-get-spooked-by-sentimentality Rohan.

The message the following morning was an apology.

'Forgive my asinine behaviour?'

'Nothing to forgive. If I can take your happy mode, I should be able to deal with this too.'

'I come with peace.'

'What peace? I'm sure you can do better than an olive branch.'

'You're negotiating my offer of peace?'

'Darn right I am. You give a girl heartache, you got to level up.'

'What do you have in mind? Tell me...'

'Hold the thought. Whenever you're in my city next...,'

'Done deal! Hey, how's the prof doing? Tell all.'

'Am being a good girl!'

'Why? I thought this trip was all about having a wild time!'

'You seem keener than I on that...'

'Sure I do. And although I'd like an up-close and personal view, for now, I'm all up for details of its "Californication"!'

The ability of this man to lighten up a situation amazed her.

'I'll try. And I'll keep in mind the up-close and personal demonstration.

Consider it my "bring back" to you from the American land.'

'In that case, can't wait for you to be back. Btw, when is that? I'm going to be in Delhi from 12th to 14th.'

'I don't get in till the 16th. Postpone your trip…'

'Can't. It's work.'

'And…you won't give me any more details about it, naturally?'

'The details are boring.'

'Try me.'

'It's a project involving the construction of apartment blocks in multiple cities. That works for now?'

'Yup! Sounds like a biggie.'

'Just pray it happens. This could change my life.'

She felt the familiar drive, the passion she was so used to by now.

'I'll always be rooting for you, you know that.'

'Yeah, I do and it's a thought I love coming home to…'

Both Amaya and Anahita were at a café in the Ferry Building Marketplace, relaxing and chatting over coffee and waffles. Amaya was nostalgic about how the time had flown. She said it seemed just yesterday that they were toddlers. They shared memories about their childhood and adolescence. The topic moved to the present and First Friday. Amaya added that she was totally taken in by the concept and how immense the experience had been. And then it struck her.

'This is it! This is the "more" that I needed in Amaya Books and More!'

'I'm listening,' said Anahita who could see the excitement on her sister's face.

'My own miniature First Friday, recreated at ABM. I could hold events in the open space outside the store,' she exclaimed as if she'd hit a gold mine. 'I mean, not all of it together, but on a one-event-at-a-time basis. Art exhibitions, photography exhibits, installations, music. Maybe even a cookout to promote a cookbook. It could give upcoming writers and artists a platform to showcase their work, giving it exposure to a wider gallery. So, there's the bookshop with its goings-on in the inside and the outside is the "MORE"—a conjunction of the creative, contemporary and tech-savvy. Blending in reading with other intellectual and creative formats and at the same time, a dynamic space that on the topmost layer is a bookstore but the underlying layers have much more to offer. The textures will breathe life into the store,' Amaya said it all in one super charged breath.

Anahita was listening to her intently, completely focusing on every excited word spoken by her sister. 'Hmmm. Well, I think you've decoded the "MORE", but what about the economics of it all?'

'Yeah, that I need to work on,' she said, laughing at her sister's ability to give her a reality check, as always.

'No, I'm not saying it can't be done,' Anahita continued. 'In fact, it all sounds brilliant, just as long as you figure out a way to make it cost-effective. Strike a deal with the artists. Tell them you're giving them the space, so they don't charge you over! They're getting patronage; some of them probably even a breakthrough.'

'True, and maybe every once in a while, I get the established and reputed lot in, who do it all for the love of their art. Pro-bono, in a sense, huh?'

'Why not? Just keep in mind that the book sales aren't overlooked. After all, you are essentially a bookstore.'

'I know what you mean, but this has to go beyond the Math. It may sound a lot to take in at a time, but if the visual can get translated into reality, then it will all be in harmony. We'll go one baby step at a time, and take it up from there.' Amaya had never been a fantasist; she lived in a world of brass-tacks so she was carefully constructing all these parallel ideas trying to work out their feasibility, negotiating with both the rational and creative aspects.

'I can't wait to get back and get it all rolling.'

The sisters looked at each other in an understanding and silence that is discernible only by two people who can read each other's mind.

Nineteen

Something was still missing. Since her return from Oakland, Amaya had several creative sessions with the architects and design team for ABM. To recreate the miniature First Friday fair was what she really wanted to do. But her visualization and realization of the arena wasn't showing through in the team's handiwork. She thought of Rohan and then hesitated, deeming it inappropriate to use his professional expertise in a personal format. Then, changing her mind according to the 'when with Rohan, think like Rohan' mantra, she messaged him, coming straight to the point.

'Hey, need a favour!'

She heard from him after a couple of hours.

'Shoot.'

'I know you're super busy and I hate to be bothersome…'

'You aren't bothersome. Now, tell me.'

From the tone of the text, it was evident that he was in the middle of work, yet he was attentive to her. That was his way of establishing her place in his life, or so she wanted to believe.

'I'm at a dead end with my bookstore plans.'

'You are? I thought it was all going smoothly.'

'Well, it is. But I just need to join in some more pieces.'

'Okay. So, what's my job?'

'I need suggestions from the architect in you. How do we do this? I can't text it to you. A trip to Delhi in the offing?'

'None that I can confirm right now. But, hey, why don't we just get on a video chat and that could be a start. Let me see what you have in mind.'

'Super! Now?'

'Gimme ten…let me wrap what's right in front of me.'

They were both at their workstations on the video call. Amaya gave him a quick brief of the modifications she required, clearly explaining the demarcation between Amaya Books and the 'More'.

'It's this creative space, the one beyond the books. That's the one I'm stuck with.' She then explained that the bookstore was moving as per plans. But she wasn't being able to intersperse it with the arty hub.

After listening to her without interrupting, he said, 'So, basically you want this whole structure to have a multidimensional, dynamic look, rather than a demarcated one.'

'Yeah, but I don't want one interfering with the other. You know what I mean?'

'Yeah, I do. You don't want to get in the way of the readers that mean business.'

'Bang on!'

'Okay. Gimme a day or two; will come up with something,' he said deep in thought and doodling away on a paper. 'Since we're on the subject, there's this other thing…the name of your bookstore.'

'Amaya Books and More? What about it?'

He raised his index finger, still in a trail of thought, and said, 'Follow me.' He juggled the phone so that a larger view of the room was visible, and moved towards a whiteboard. He scribbled three options on it:

AMAYA BOOKS

and MORE—option 1

AMAYA BOOKS and MORE—option 2

AMAYA THE BOOKSTORE and MORE—option 3

He turned around, addressing her, 'Well?'

Amaya was puzzled for a few seconds, but as soon as she fathomed what he was getting at, her gaze was transfixed on the board. All three read differently to the mind and the eye.

'You'd obviously want the headboard to read one way or the other,' Rohan added.

'Yes, yes, I would. I need to think on this one,' she said, still staring at the options.

'Damn! Now I've given you something more to think about!' he said, with his hands in his pockets, looking helpless at the development. 'Anyway, you take your time, and do your thinking. And before you go thanking me incessantly, you're welcome!'

'This is probably the first time I've caught you in thinking mode,' Amaya said laughingly.

He looked straight at her via the camera, 'This is me in my work zone.' And then, he gave his trademark shrug with his head tilted to one side. 'But you are just too distracting for me to stay like this for too long,' he said with a boyish smile.

'And you have blown my mind!'

'Your mind, your mind...we can't afford to have that blown. By the way, you look good in those specs.'

'Thanks! So, you're going to get back to me?'

'Yep, will do. And now, as much as I don't want to, I need to get going for a meeting,' he gave her a long gaze and ran his fingers on her lips. 'Ciao'.

She had her homework cut out for her. The ABM logo needed a rethink, and a good one at that. Amaya cursed herself for not checking with Rohan on his choice of the three, but realized he may not have spoken his mind on that one till she did. She let the effect of his fingers touching her lips, albeit, through the phone, linger on.

Twenty

$\mathcal{A}$maya was in the bookstore supervising the furniture that had just arrived. It had been a busy week. Rohan had emailed her a few suggestions and she was toying with them to get the best fit. As was typical of him, he had gone incommunicado. But she was used to his way of working. And as expected, out of the blue, she got a text at the end of the working day.

'Long fucking day!'

'Story of your life. How goes it?'

'Labouring! Nine to nine! Just too much going on. Need to wrap up a project and I'm simultaneously pitching for the new one. It's a big deal and I want it clinched, the prep-work is a killer.'

'Hmmm…so the stress meter's burning hot?'

'Always! But that's enough dope on my non-existent play life. What's up with you?'

'The bookstore! That's what my life is all about these days. You know, that point you made about using the open space into the creative end? That is what I'm working on.'

'Glad to be of help.'

'And talking of "play life", I'm off to Goa next weekend. It's Mihir's fortieth birthday on the 31st.'

'Nice! Goa…the sun, sand, beach, you in a bikini!'

'You got it!'

'I'm envious!'

'Hey…why don't you join us?'

'Didn't you just read? I'm swamped with my to-do list.'

'It's just two days. And it's a weekend! Get away and I guarantee you; it'll be therapeutic, amongst other things…'

'What's the "other things"?'

'See them for yourself!'

'But, seriously babe, I can't just crash the party?'

'You're not crashing it! You're invited! We reach on the 30th, spend two crazy nights and days partying and you can be back on Monday. C'mon. Give yourself the "thinkless" you keep preaching me about.'

'I'd have to leave first thing Monday morning.'

'You can pull it off dude, you know that.'

'Well, the thought is tempting. I'd give anything to be with a bikini-clad you! God knows I could do with the break, going crazy here.'

'I take that as an affirmative. Mailing you the invite…see you in Goa!'

Okay. So, she had just invited Rohan to Goa—just like that! She called Mihir with the update. Mihir was delighted. He joked that it was about time her 'text'ual intercourse got sexual. He reassured her that it was a fabulous idea. Amaya stopped hyperventilating, slowly warming to the fact that it would be something to have him with her. All at once, there was so much more to look forward to on this trip.

Twenty-one

*G*oa. Amaya and Noor had planned everything for the momentous occasion. After checking into the hotel and taking timeout to prep for the evening, they made their way to a popular restaurant, a five-minute drive from the hotel. The spot was known for its breathtaking view of the sunset.

Amaya's phone beeped and she knew it was what she was waiting for.

'Hey, just landed! See you soon…start missing me!'

'Missing you already! Get here soon before I can't bear it any longer.'

'I like that already.'

'You haven't seen nothing yet!'

'True that! I haven't…'

The mood was leisurely and celebratory. The afterglow of the sky diffused its warmth to the expanse. 'There is something sensual about a scenic sunset. It thaws the skin and penetrates within,' Amaya spoke her thoughts out aloud.

'Yeah, it is an irresistible sight,' added Noor, cozying up to Mihir, who was capturing the scenes on his camera.

Amaya was desperately waiting for Rohan to arrive. She was longing to be with him, feel his presence next to her—a feeling that had visited her ever so often since their brief time together in Mumbai. Rohan brought out a different spirit in her. His exuberance and boyish charm, the offhand bent of mind and his focus; his casual but definitive concern for her; his intimacy one moment and withdrawal the next—all of it had kept her guessing many a times. But she was ready to take whatever she could get from him, no conditions applied.

He arrived, wearing a white half-sleeved shirt, khaki cargos, flip-flops and the quintessential 'Rohan' stubble, shades perched on the crown of his head. He walked up to Amaya and gave her a long warm hug. The moment their bodies touched, a now recognizable innervation encapsulated her body. 'You just missed the sunset,' she said to him.

His eyes didn't leave her face. 'No, I didn't,' he said, running his fingers through her hair, his eyes looking deeply into hers. 'Your hair looks different babe, it's longer. I like it like this.' She was pleasantly surprised at his keen observation. Rohan did a quick and appreciative top to bottom scan of the woman in front of him, who was in a simple white tube sundress and contrasting orange-hued accessories. She introduced him to Noor and Mihir. The two men hit it off instantly which didn't really come as a surprise to Amaya. They were both unaffected, easygoing people.

The evening kicked off; Amaya was busy socializing and ensuring that Mihir's countdown to his fortieth birthday was a memorable one. She divided her time between the guests and Rohan who fit in well with everybody. Totally at ease, he was quite the charmer and she noticed some of the female guests ogling at him. It was a perfect evening—going exactly the way she and Noor had envisioned over the last few weeks, and it was even better because Rohan was there with her—for her.

As dusk turned into night, the party was in full swing. The

weather was breezy and cool. Amaya looked for Rohan. From the moment he had entered, he had pretty much taken over the event. Everyone knew him by then, he had mingled with all the singles, and magically, was by her side before she could wonder where he was. It was a relief to her that she didn't have to spend her time and energy making him feel like a part of the group. He had proven competent enough to do the needful.

She spotted him behind the bar assisting the bartender in concocting cocktails for the many takers. Amaya knew that it was a tough call to be anywhere but next to him, and any attempt to pretend to do so was futile. She walked up to the bar and watched his cocktail-making skills. On seeing her, he walked up to her, held her by her waist and led her towards an empty table.

'I didn't know your skills extended to behind the bar,' Amaya said playfully.

'I can perform anywhere, darl. As for the bar, what can I say? The other me is a bartender!' He said handing her a Rohan-special cocktail.

'That's an interesting drift...a bartender!'

'Yeah! Conjuring up spirits—another way to make people happy.'

'You have a point. And this is good.' She lifted her citrus-infused cocktail.

'It has your poison in it. So what's your wild side all about? I know you have one, courtesy, that fateful California eve.'

'Oh! Don't remind me of that one!'

'Why the heck not? I loved every bit of it. So, you were saying, the wild child in you...?'

'I don't really know...never given it a thought.'

'Give it one now.'

'Hmmm...let's see,' she took a few minutes and said, 'a

gypsy maybe? Wander, seek new places, and discover myself along the way.'

'Footloose and fancy-free? That's a far cry from the publisher Amaya I know.'

'Yeah, I am pretty conventional, aren't I? But there is that bohemian spirit in the other me, I guess.'

'Will your other self appear today?'

'You wish! Hey, it's almost twelve!' She rushed to be next to Mihir and Noor and got the birthday fuss going. Amaya knew that Mihir was a special gift to her; having him as a constant, unconditionally, gave her life that extra richness. She got emotional and it became very obvious from her tight birthday hug to him. Rohan too gave Mihir a big hug.

'You two are really close, aren't you?' Rohan asked Amaya.

'Mihir and me? Yes, he's my special one and I'm blessed to have him in my life.'

'As I am to have you in mine.' The unexpected declaration caught her unawares. It was so unlike him to say anything even close to sentimental.

'Rohan Kashyap, is that you saying this? That is the nicest thing you've ever said to me!' she beamed.

Their eyes met and he was gazing at her with a look she couldn't decipher; it seemed as if there was something more he wanted to say, but almost immediately, his expression changed to a far more familiar one as he winked at her and said in a drunken drawl, 'Indulging you is one of my favourite pastimes.'

Amaya got the drift. That was all the emotion she would get from him for the time being. Rohan was back at the bar and had suitably impressed a group of Mihir's model friends that seemed ready to paw every bit of him. Amaya could hardly blame them, considering that every inch of her own body was so turned on by this avatar. He either seemed to have read her mind or had the same thought running in his, as he was by her side that very instant. The party ended on a high with Mihir giving all his friends a toast and thanking them for being with him that evening.

They got back to the hotel and Amaya could tell that while in the bartending mode, Rohan had tasted every drink he was concocting. He was tipsy and she told him that she'd walk him back to his room. He fumbled with the key card and Amaya opened the door and got him in. Plonking himself on to the bed, Rohan kicked off his shoes. He pulled her towards him and said, 'Whoops! Seems like I OD'd on the bartending bit.' Amaya sat down next to him and he placed his head on her lap, his fingers drunkenly fiddling with her hair and face. She ran her fingers on his chest. He was even more irresistible in his inebriated state.

Rohan was babbling incoherently, something about him wanting her to stay with him forever, not leave his side, wanting to touch every part of her. He turned his face towards her midriff and lightly caressed her back through her dress. She wanted him to pull the damn dress off her. She made him sit up. They kissed passionately, but his drunken state got the better of him. She watched helplessly as an intimate moment turned into a hopeless one. A passed-out Rohan lay on her lap. She tried to wake him up, but couldn't. Of all the possible permutations she had foreseen for the evening, the current one had not been one. It was time to play mommy, so she did just that. She tucked him in. She wanted him so bad. This had got to be the mother of all bummers!

Amaya sauntered back to her room in a desperate need to calm down her impassioned self. Undressing, she gazed at herself in the mirror and sighed. So much for the lacy lingerie she had put on. Piya and she had shopped for it especially for a 'Rohan' night. It had been Piya's brainwave since Amaya's wardrobe didn't boast of too many sexy things. The lacy tubes and thongs had been purchased for *the* moment. One such moment had just crashed out with a fervent foreplay being its highlight. That was that. Rohan Kashyap had left her high and dry.

Twenty-two

*A*maya surfaced late morning. While sipping the much-needed strong coffee, her mind replayed the disastrous sequence of events of the previous night. She frowned but couldn't help but be moonstruck by the out-of-control Rohan. He had looked so vulnerable lying on her lap, making drunken confessionals. It was the most intimate moment they had shared thus far.

She changed into her aquamarine-coloured bikini, tied her favourite floral sarong a little below the navel and headed for the poolside. The guests were lounging in and around the pool and further on the deck—a platform that overlooked the beach.

Noor called out to her.

'So, how was it?' she asked, with Mihir eagerly listening on.

'It was a no-show.' She gave them an edited recap.

'Men!' was Noor's terse response.

Mihir was clutching his sides and going hysterical. 'This is hilarious!'

'Yes, go ahead, laugh at my expense,' Amaya said with a grumpy face.

'Well, you still have all of today; just ensure that all he drinks today is milk and not a drop of alcohol.'

'MIHIRR! That's not funny at all!'

'Chill babe, you know I love you. Don't let this bring you

down. Like you always say, no man is going to rain on your parade.'

'True as that might be, one man is doing that very often now,' she said.

'Where is he?' Noor asked. Amaya shrugged. There was no sign of him. Amaya wondered if she should check on him. Just then, she got a text from him.

'I slept on you and literally this time! That too, with my clothes on! Something tells me I was a colossal screwup last night.'

'You were quite an act! Feeling okay?'

'Hungover! Be with you in half an hour.'

Rohan was there in forty minutes, wearing a light blue linen shirt and white bermudas. 'And I thought you'd spend the day sleeping!' Amaya said to him.

He looked at her from top to bottom, and said, 'You sure are a sight for sore eyes. About sleeping, this is not the way I had imagined spending a night with you, so how many "sorrys" will make a worthy apology?'

'Hey, it's cool. Don't worry about it.'

She was amazed at her ability to deal with the situation at hand, but it had been the need of the hour. She needed to maintain a balance between detachment and concern. At the right moment, she would reveal to him his sentimental babbling from the previous night. Maybe use it as a trump card the next time he rendered a discourse on getting emotionally spooked.

It was a resplendent, sunny morning. Rohan and Amaya got into the pool, Rohan not leaving Amaya's side even for a second. He was playing with her hair, running his fingers on her body, with his arms around her waist almost always. Amaya was no longer in touch with the backdrop, for her, it was just the two of them. At some point, Rohan got out of the pool, held his hand to help her out, and they walked off to her room.

He made a dash to his room while Amaya waited for him. He came back with his shirt off, moved next to her, and swooped down to her lips. Almost rhythmically, he lifted her onto the bed. He unclasped her bikini top and smoothly pulled down the bottom while kissing her mouth. He held her breasts, and nuzzled them, sucking on them gently. It was a sexual high for Amaya as nothing aroused her more. She undressed him. He had an erection, hard and firm. They took turns being on top, every inch of their bodies craving for more.

The lovemaking was overpowering. As they were about to climax, Rohan whispered to her, 'Hold me tight, Amaya.' She responded and they came together. He stayed in her for a few seconds while she stroked his hair. They remained in each other's arms till they were satiated.

'Babe, you were awesome!' Rohan said as they lay in bed.

'We were awesome, Rohan, in that space called "us",' she replied.

He gazed at her but didn't say anything further. She wanted him to. She wanted to know how it was for him, but she also knew that he wouldn't say a word more on that. He told Amaya that he was going to call it a night since he was flying out first thing in the morning and the next day was a crucial one at work. He didn't reveal any more details; he didn't like to talk about his work. She knew and understood that. Submerged in her happy place, she kissed him goodnight.

When Amaya woke up the next morning, Rohan had already left, as was expected. She read his message.

'Thank you for giving me a memorable weekend. Apologies for my immature drunk shenanigan, and I hope you'll believe me when I say that

leaving you this morning was a tough call. Btw, take a look at your lips.
I've planted a kiss on them.'

As a reflex action, she moved her tongue on her lips and felt the rush from the previous night.

She texted him.

'It was magical Rohan! Thank you for being with me and I hope you will believe me when I say that I miss you already. Being without you is going to be a tougher call.'

She then punched in 'xx'.

On the flight back to Delhi, Amaya slipped into her own world and smiled to herself, thinking about the night with Rohan. They had been swell in bed, as they were together outside it and in the virtual world. He'd called her 'awesome'. 'Awesome', the all-encompassing one-word-says-it-all adjective! Once something or someone had awesome prefixed, the rest was either self-explanatory or left to the imagination. So, their time together and her performance in bed were summed up in that one word. She would have liked to talk more about their time together, to know more about how he had felt with her. But she'd have to make do with 'awesome' for now. She laughed to herself—a different case of performance anxiety this was.

Her night with Tarun had to be a two, compared to Rohan's ten on a scale of one to ten. The one thing she was certain of was that she had left Rohan wanting more; no matter how much of a player he was, this time she'd played coach. No mush, no emotional melodrama, just one step at a time had to be her mantra.

Twenty-three

Amaya chatted with her parents and told them about the 'awesome' Goa celebration. It was close to nine in the night when she heard from Rohan.

'My bad! Been at that presentation prep up all day! It's gonna take a couple more hours of the night too.'

By now Amaya was well-aware that his work tone was different from his 'leisure' tone and this one was clearly the former. Going with the same flow, she texted back.

'Hey, it will be kickass! I know you…you won't have it any other way.'

If only she was better clued in on what the presentation was all about, she would have had better stuff to say than this generic show of solidarity.

'Babe, I'm spooked. This is *the* biggest thing I've ever done!'

She was tempted to add 'Aah you get spooked in other ways too' but resisted it and instead sent a reassuring message.

'It'll all be good, Rohan. Don't think too much!'

'Hah! I karmically deserve that one, eh?'

'Just trying to destress those nerves. '

'Thanks 'darl! Need to get back…later.'

Amaya got back to the board life she had been out of for quite some time. After spending an hour playing, she turned in for the night as she had a long day ahead of her. Wondering whether Rohan was still at work, she messaged.

'You're going to kick ass, I'm so sure of it!'

Amaya's day went by with the supervision of the bookstore. The bookshelves were in place. She had chosen textured floor-length curtains with a neutral colour scheme. The flooring was done in terracotta-coloured stone tiles. Fully upholstered floral print sofas were kept in the reading lounge.

A winding wooden staircase led to the first floor. The café still needed work. A handwritten menu on a blackboard was all she had for now. Wrought iron square tables and chairs had been ordered. The remaining area had the same décor as the ground floor. One end of it was designed for the children's workshops with brightly painted orange workstations and funky stationery. The other part was lined with big and small bookshelves that surrounded an empty space, which would convert into the authors' meet. An aesthetically done powder room completed the premises. It was turning out pretty much as she had envisaged.

Things had changed for Amaya post Goa. No matter how effectively she tried to keep on a strictly 'no strings attached' basis with Rohan, their affinity had stirred up an emotion or two to surface. She couldn't get him off her mind; she didn't want to. The calmness the very thought of Rohan brought to her being was worth every bit.

'I kicked ass!'

His text read after what she assumed was a presentation gone well.

'And…?'

'Well…unofficially, we're there. Officially, I'll know next week.'

'That's super! Now, do you think you can give me some dope on what I've been rooting for?'

'Babe, you've been so awesome about this. It's no big secret. Just that I don't like to talk about my work. It isn't as interesting as yours, just boring buildings.'

In time, Amaya would need to make him understand that she was all ears for his trials, tribulations and triumphs, both personal and professional. But for now, she would stick to playing a devoted morale booster.

'We call it unconditional support, disclosure notwithstanding.'

'Will tell you all. In fact, post the meeting in Delhi, I'm all yours. And all I want is for you to be all mine, since unconditional support is your USP.'

'Then, make that trip ASAP. I'd love for you to see how the bookstore is shaping up.'

'That's it? That should be my only incentive?'

'Well, I am using my powers of persuasion to get you here.'

'You hold the power to convert a three incher into a nine incher just by your touch. That's persuasion too…and a powerful one at that!'

'Oh! That's an easy one.'

'No, not that easy. Not everyone can "persuade" me that way.'

'Then I take it as a compliment! So, does that mean I see you soon?'

'I'll try…will work out something. Can't say no to a pretty girl's request.'

Twenty-four

*I*t was a thought that had crossed her mind a few times. Amaya called Raina over to the office for a professional offer she had for her. The two women got along well, and had stayed in touch despite their busy schedules. Raina told her she wanted to chat about her personal life. But first things first; Amaya put forth her proposition to Raina.

'I have a job offer for you. I want you to take over the entire creative aspect, or as I call it, the "more" of ABM.'

Raina looked completely disconcerted. 'Amaya, you don't have to do this for me.'

'Not at all. The way I see it, you're the right person for the job.' She added that Raina's profile and experience at her current job could be used to its optimum at ABM. She would need to plan and organize a creative event every month and oversee its smooth running from start to finish. 'We will discuss it beforehand. Let's say, we just follow the leads on art, photography, music and anything and everything that can evoke our interest. We then invite them to exhibit or perform here. The USP has to be untouched, new and unrecognized talent. The deal would be that since they need a platform to showcase themselves, we provide it to them free of cost or at something nominal. That way, ABM doesn't need to invest much in that sphere.'

'It's a fantastic idea, Amaya. But I'm not sure I can take up the responsibility. I mean, I still have my bad days.'

'I'm willing to bet my money on you. If you do this right, there's no looking back for you. If you fuck up, then you get fired, like any regular employee would. Think about it. You have a month to decide.'

'I don't need a month. It's a yes.'

Amaya discussed Raina's salary with her, which in itself was enough for her to agree—it was nearly double of her current take-home. Yes, it was a gamble—Amaya knew that, but it could also just be the chance Raina needed.

She needed to get into a meeting. Looking at her watch, she said to Raina, 'Hey, what was the personal matter you wanted to discuss?'

'I can see you're busy, so we'll do that another time.' Raina thanked her again for the offer and promised that she would get back to her very soon.

Twenty-five

$\mathcal{I}$t was an evening out at a rooftop restaurant at a South Delhi mall. Amaya had just reached when she ran into Virat Bakshi.

'Hey there, stranger!' Before she could say anything, he scooped to embrace her and planted a peck half on her lips and half on her cheek.

Amaya gently pushed him away and said, 'You seem to be in a happy mode!'

'Yeah! Life's good and I'm happy. Now, happier to see you, sexy.'

'Where's Rupali? Let me go say hi to her.' Amaya tried bringing him back to 'Planet Wife'. She could tell he was eye-fucking her. 'Oh! She couldn't make it. Samaira wasn't feeling too good,' Virat replied, referring to their daughter.

'I'm heading for a drink.' She left before he could respond.

The rest of the evening was a merry-go-round with Amaya trying to tactfully dodge Virat. He was aggressive, making his lust for her obvious. While she was with a couple of other friends, he sidled up to her, put his arm around her waist and said, 'You shouldn't be getting your own drinks, lady. I'm at your service.'

To those not in the know, it seemed like an innocuous, extremely chivalrous gesture. What was unseen was Virat's arm casually resting on her waist, moving around her back, gently stroking it and further sliding down. Amaya was uncomfortable, not just on the account that it could be noticed by an observant eye, but more so because she didn't want him to touch any part of her. She thanked him and moved to meet a few more friends. He probably read this as a sign to carry on, because soon enough, he was by her side, with her drink in his hand.

'Virat darling, so good to see you!' crooned a voice from behind. A shapely young woman was next to him and that gave Amaya the much-needed escape route.

'I'll catch you later, Virat. Cheers!' she signalled to him, endorsing the presence of his new companion. It had to stop! It was beyond tease now. There was unease. Yes, a moment had taken place between them many moons ago. But surely, the man needn't hold on to it for a lifetime? He needed to get over that golden moment. Whatever attraction she had felt for him fleetingly was long gone. In her defence, she hadn't given Virat any overtures for him to take forward. What was it? Her body language? Her looks? Why did he continue to assume that Amaya wanted him?

Amaya believed there was way too much baggage in the married-man zone. She neither needed it nor wanted to unpack any of it. That was the reason she always steered clear of triangular entrapments. The trouble was that the men wouldn't blink an eyelid before covering their own asses and blaming it all on the 'single bitch'. Most wives would uphold the testimony, and in cases where the dalliance worked, it still remained messy. She would figure a way out soon. Maybe the next time Rohan was around, she would flaunt him and ensure Virat got an eyeful and hopefully back off. It wasn't a foolproof plan, but worth giving a shot.

Back at work the next morning, it was all about ABM. Rohan sent in some vital inputs, but Amaya would've liked him to see the premises which he also reckoned was a better plan. She wanted him, wanted to be with him—that was a given now.

She then got a call from him.

'Hey you, what's up?' she asked, surprised as they normally messaged. It was quite unlike him to call.

'How are you placed Wednesday–Thursday?' He came straight to the point without any formalities.

'Umm,' she paused, mentally connecting to the next two days, 'just busy with ABM and usual stuff, maybe a night out. Tell me?'

'Can't give you the exact details, but I'll be in Delhi Wednesday morning, some last-minute snag with the project...'

'Snag? That doesn't sound right.'

'Nah, not really a snag. It's just some formality that got overlooked. Anyway, so I should be done latest by the evening, and in case you're still up for me to come by the store and my bonus thereafter, then I will extend my trip by another day.'

'In case I'm up for it? Rohan? Of course I am!'

'Super! Let's touch base soon then? Be available for me any time after six,' he said in an authoritative yet protective tone.

Twenty-six

'*G*ood for you, Amu.' Amaya's best girl was happy that she'd be meeting her man again. 'This must be a sign. The stars must've finally aligned.'

Amaya stopped herself from getting into the same debate again, with Piya calling her 'thing' with Rohan a relationship and Amaya disaffirming the proclamation. Instead, she good-humouredly chatted about his impending trip.

'I just hope he can make time to come by the site.'

Things were progressing, but she felt it was the right time for him to suggest modifications. Strange! It wasn't as if she had seen any of his work. She only had her judgement to rely on. Talk about being biased! Wednesday was going to be a full-on ABM day. One, Amaya had an important meeting lined up with the interiors team and the children's section needed finalization.

Two, it was regarding the organic green tea/coffee she wanted developed as an exclusive brand for the store. Avantika Mittal had started her own line of 'healthy organic food'. Amaya had thrown the idea to her, and the rich father's young, enthusiastic daughter, keen to prove herself with her new line of business, had jumped at it. Amaya hoped that Avantika had inherited her father's business acumen.

Three, the ABM logo.

Four, perusing the list emailed by Raina, who was now on

board, compiling her choices for the 'events and more'.

Around six, heading for her workout, she messaged Rohan.

'What's up? What's the plan?'

She hadn't heard from him, except for the reconfirmation of his being in Delhi as planned. Clearly, with him, nothing could be assumed. He was so exasperating. She awaited a reply from Rohan so she could plan the rest of the evening. It was not before nine-thirty that she finally heard from him.

'Hey, all done now. Flight got delayed, and so did the rest of the day. I'm with my client for a drink. Why don't you join us?'

'Client? Hey, you carry on. Not in a mood for too much company.'

'I thought so. You wouldn't be interested in this kinda evening and I'm stuck. This guy is helluva party-man! But I'm on your time tomorrow onwards. When should I reach your office?'

'Onwards, as in?'

'As in, with you, for you, till as long as you want.'

What more could be said? This project meant the world to Rohan, so in the scheme of things she really couldn't say or do much was thought number one. He'd appeased her already by making up for his absence today by a compensatory one for the next day. Men really knew how to play it. They always had their next move planned was thought number two. She decided to go with the first thought.

'Tomorrow, it is then!'

True to his word, Rohan was at the Amaya Books office at sharp noon. He walked into her room, and turning to ensure that the door was shut, embraced her uninhibitedly. He held on to her and kissed her.

'Damn! I've missed you Amaya!' His apparent warmth was a bona fide exhibit of his declaration.

'Where to from here?' he asked releasing her from his tight grasp. Amaya, still under the effect of the lip lock and his nearness, conferred a completely different meaning of his words and replied, 'Wherever you want to go.'

'Babe, then let's head to the site! I wanna see what you've been up to.' There! Her cue to come down to 'Planet Here and Now'.

'Sure! Give me a minute. Tea? Coffee?'

'Just you,' He flashed his irresistible smile.

Shooting off a few instructions to Radhika and the other staff, she led Rohan to the ground floor.

'This is it. All yours!'

The transformation of 'Rohan the man' to 'Rohan the architect' was instant. Inspecting the open space where the events were to take place, he exclaimed, 'Oh Amaya! There's so much you can do with this space. Show me the plan for this one.' Next, he was studying the assigned layout.

'I'm glad you're keeping this space green to whatever extent possible. Gives it more texture.'

'This is mom's baby. She's got a green thumb. The landscaping is her virtuoso work.'

Even after they moved base to their Jorbagh home and this house was converted into Amaya Books, Neena Kapoor had retained the green patch. She would visit often, instructing the gardener and making sure that her suggestions of plants were adhered to. Hence, ever since the conception of ABM, Amaya was clear that the area would be landscaped under her supervision.

'You should make full use of it!'

'In the winter months, yes we will. But you know Delhi summers. No one would want to be here then.'

'Hmm. We'll think of something, but through the good months as you call them, keep this place alive. Do you have that planned? Because all landscaping will have to happen accordingly.'

'The events—they will happen here.'

'Nah, not just that. That would make it all too space-specific. You need to keep juggling. Extend the bookstore here…to the outside.'

'Huh? You lost me.'

'Keep a couple of bookshelves of bestsellers or new arrivals, or something else thematic out here. Let your readers relish the Delhi winter on the days sans an event. Maybe you could have one of those author-meets here.' Amaya could see that Rohan had studied the email she had sent him. He continued, completely immersed in brainwork, 'Have a chai-stall here,' referring to the indigenous tea cart, a familiar sight on Delhi roads.

'Hmmm…a kitschy-looking one,' went Amaya, in tandem with Rohan's words.

'It'll brighten up the place. Don't overdo it. That would take away from the space here,' he grabbed her hand and continued, 'let's see what you have inside.'

The suggestions kept coming, making Amaya feel like hiring him officially. He suggested that an alternate 'exhibit area' should be conceptualized indoors too, keeping the hot/rainy months in mind. He complimented her on the bookstore section. According to him, it meant business and yet was inviting enough for people to stop by.

'Enough for now. Watch this space for more!' he pointed to himself.

'The genius that is Rohan,' she said glancing at her diary, noting down the last suggestion.

'Tell me something new! And now can a man satiate his thirst and hunger?' Rohan said in a tone that suggested he was alluding to more than just food and drink.

'Uh! Look at me! All caught up in this marathon of mine,' Amaya looked at her watch and realized it was nearly three. 'Let me make a quick round upstairs, and then let's get out of here?'

'And I thought you'd never ask! You go, wrap up your day, I'll just go through my mails and stuff and make a call or two.'

'Where to?' Amaya asked Rohan, once they were both seated in the car.

'How about the hotel? We could just order room service and...' he moved his hand to push her hair behind her ear.

'Ya, let's,' she said. He instructed the driver to take them to the hotel where he was staying.

It was obvious. They both wanted each other. As soon as they were in the room, it all happened with neither one of them having the power to savour foreplay. Amaya climaxed over and over again, each time wanting the next orgasm to give her more release, and Rohan was turned on enough to satisfy her till she was spent.

'Six in a row, superwoman!' Rohan said. 'You're a tough one to satisfy!'

'Whoever said I was easy?' she replied cagily. 'And you performed well. Full marks!'

'Yeah, I came through, didn't I?' he said with a wink.

They ordered room service and kept the banter going over the meal. It was time for her to get going. 'I have my workout scheduled for seven-thirty, but I don't think I'll be able to make it.'

'You need to work out more? Give me some time, I'll match up to your stamina soon. And I haven't had enough of you yet. Do you really need to go?'

'I don't want to, but I need to be home, at least briefly.'

They made plans for the night. 'What are you in a mood for?' Amaya asked him before leaving, so she could plan ahead.

'More of you! And maybe some music, malt and the pleasure of seeing you dance to my tune.'

'Perfect!'

'I've heard the hotel bar is good. What say?' Rohan hugged her from behind and rested his chin on her shoulder. Amaya placed her hand on the nape of his neck.

'It is but I want you to get out of the hotel. Hauz Khas Village has it all too. It's not my fav haunt, but this new place there should meet your requisites. How about I meet you here in the lobby by nine?'

'Nine it is!'

Her mom was in the garden and Amaya told her that Rohan was in town. 'He came by the office today, to look around and throw some more ideas. He's an architect, you know, so…'

'Yes, baby, I do know he's the architect,' she replied as if to remind her that she had been given this information time and again.

'We're going out for dinner tonight as he's off tomorrow. Should be back by one-ish.'

'Have fun and take care,' her mother said and Amaya went off to her room to get ready. Piya had been calling and texting. Amaya showered and gave her a lowdown while getting dressed.

'What? No way! Already? So, it's round two then tonight?' Piya was cracking up on the phone, loving every bit of teasing her best friend.

'Not a bad idea!' Amaya played along.

'Hey, why don't Atul and you join us?' she said as she got into another one of her black dresses.

'And see you pawing each other? Thank you but no. I want you to make the most of your time with him. Next time, maybe. He's all yours tonight.'

Twenty-seven

$\mathcal{A}$maya messaged Rohan from the hotel lobby. He was down in a couple of minutes looking dapper in jeans and an electric blue shirt. They headed for HKV and once there, Amaya showed him around.

'I love this place!' Rohan said looking as fascinated as he sounded. 'It's such a maze to get from one alley to the other!'

'This was a favourite hangout during college; then it just disappeared from the map of Delhi. It was resurrected recently and now there's no stopping it.' Amaya filled him in, playing the tourist guide. 'The next time you're here, we'll come during the day. It's a whole new world then.'

'Yeah! Looks like my trips to Delhi are going to get more frequent.' She knew he was referring to the big new project, but before Amaya could broach it any further, they reached the pub and the conversation was lost.

'Cool place!' said Rohan. 'I like this island bar.'

They moved on the first level through the staircase that had ropes suspended in place of a railing. Rohan was scanning the place. 'Whoa! This look is so different from the one downstairs,' referring to the all-wood look with hard wooden chairs and benches kept as seating.

'I hope you like the live band, too,' Amaya asked him in anticipation.

'Hell yes! I sure do love live performances. You should know that by now!' he replied laughingly.

'Vodka for my soul. You take your pick,' Amaya said glancing through the drinks menu. He ordered a malt whisky.

'Soul, eh? The body satiated itself?'

'For the time being, yes it did. No saying for how long though. Hey, why are you so secretive about this deal of yours? You can trust me, I won't tell,' she jibed.

'I trust you blindly. And really, this "deal" isn't that big a deal. Especially for a bigwig like you who cracks one a day!'

'What makes you say that? I'm no bigwig! That said, this is the biggest deal of your life; I've been there. I know what it feels like,' Amaya said downplaying her career graph with the aim of making his moment seem sizeable.

'Always...the right words, the perfect drift! Rest assured that when the time cometh, you will be the first to know,' he placed his hands on hers.

'I better be!'

They chatted comfortably and discovered more about each other in the process. It hit Amaya that she wanted to spend more and more time with Rohan in a real space. She then asked him how Guy was doing. 'I had asked her for a little to-do regarding Rajbir. Wonder if she remembers?' she said.

'Here's her number. Check with her anytime. She's pretty much Rajbir's blue-eyed girl, so she would know,' Rohan said.

Amaya needed to follow up on Rajbir's memoirs vociferously. Last she had checked, he was abroad on location for a two-month long shoot. She made a note of rechecking the very next morning. The live band was indeed 'awesome' as Rohan said and after a couple of snacks, he led Amaya to the makeshift dance floor and they danced holding each other very close. Amaya was lost in him. She moved with his body and he moved to hers.

Then abruptly, Rohan said, 'Let's get the hell out of here.' His breath was heavy and short. Back in the cab, both of them were high on alcohol and each other. Amaya was conscious of the cab driver in the front seat, but Rohan seemed oblivious of his presence. He kissed her and his being off guard made her throw caution to the wind. They made out till they were a couple of minutes away from her place.

'Do you have any idea how much you turn me on?' he said to her as the cab halted in front of her house.

'Would you like to come in for a cuppa? My folks are home, so that's all there is on the menu!' Amaya asked, not having had a fill of him yet.

'Sure! But I ain't responsible for my actions!'

'Since when did you become a disclaimer?' Amaya teased him, fully intending the wordplay.

'Told you, you're addictive.'

He asked the cabbie to wait for an hour and they took the staircase outside the house up to Amaya's living area. She went into the pantry and put together two cups of green tea. The awareness of her folks being just a floor below must have also passed on to Rohan. He sat on the couch and kept a respectable distance from her, only allowing his hand to move through her hair and neck.

'You love doing this, don't you?' Amaya asked him.

'Yeah! It soothes my fractured soul…'

'Why do you keep saying that?' she asked.

'Long story. Nothing too dramatic though.'

'Old love?'

'Yeah, something like that, but not at all relevant right here, right now.' Amaya didn't persist. Everyone had a past. It was the past that gave the next time around more potential.

'Your store's shaping up really well, Retro!'

'You think?' Amaya asked, as she was keen on every word of endorsement on her dream project.

'Yup! Make it happen to Delhi...'

After chatting for a little while, Rohan got up to leave. He gave her a kiss. Amaya wanted to hold on to the moment forever.

Twenty-eight

'Mihir and you? Since when? What?' Amaya was visibly stunned by Raina's confession.

'Since that night at Gymkhana actually. We just hit it off and kept in touch, you know, texting and stuff,' Raina replied.

'And?'

'And then we met a few times, and then, well yes, to answer your obvious query, the sex is on. I need it every once a while and he's ready for it too. By the way, we're great in bed!' Raina's face was beaming with pleasure and fulfilment.

'Where does Noor fit into all this?'

'That is not my concern, Amaya. She's for Mihir to handle. What I do know is that the arrangement is working suitably for me.'

'Arrangement! So that's how the new-age fuck buddies defined three-way relationships,' Amaya thought to herself. She wondered why Mihir hadn't mentioned the new development to her. The consternation on her face must have been obvious as Raina added, 'Don't think so much about it, Amaya. I know it's not your kind of thing, but it works for me. That man Mihir is a dreamboat. I just can't get enough of him, if you know what I mean.' Raina winked.

'And you're all right with him sleeping with Noor, too?'

'I don't give a flying fuck about what he does with Noor

or more like her. He's there when I need him and the way I need him. That is all that matters to me.'

'Why didn't you tell me? About Raina and you?' Amaya asked Mihir. They were catching up over a drink at a restobar in Khan Market.

'What's there to tell, sweetheart? Your friend has a voracious sexual appetite and I'm a horny bastard. That sums it up.'

'And Noor?'

'Noor has her freedom too. You know that. Whether or not she exercises it is up to her. Amaya, everything goes in today's world. Do you know they have online apps these days where friends can find friends to bang? Which world are you living in?'

'There's an online app for everything these days. And there is a world beyond yours, Mihir. This happy bubble you're living in is going to burst someday, you know that, don't you? One of them is going to fall in love with you if they haven't already and the drama will begin. Then, we'll talk.'

'In that case you better be prepared to play agony aunt. Chances are you'll be the first person either of the two will come running to. Till then, I'm a happy chappy and let's keep it to that.' Mihir put his arm around her and said, 'No one replaces you. You're way too smart for the bullshit, Amaya.'

Amaya was convinced that she was outdated. When and how did all this happen? Why was she left so far behind these modern mechanisms and analogies? She sure was differently abled when it came to all this. And to think she had always considered herself a sexually liberated woman!

It had been a week since Rohan had left. Amaya had already put his suggestions into action. After much deliberation, she had decided to stick to 'Amaya Books and More' as the name of the store. Raina had sent in the options for the logo designs; she had become an inseparable component of ABM now and was officially on board of the soon-to-open boutique bookstore.

Amaya did her daily scan of the site. Her vision was finally coming alive. The lawn had not been manicured to give it a more natural and homely feel, rather than a landscaped one. The old trees and some plants were retained, keeping in mind ABM's endeavour to 'keep it green'. That was the new addition to the whole outfit—carry-bags made of newspaper, earthenware mugs sourced from potters straight from the villages in Barmer, and the green space. The concept had started with retaining the lawn to reduce the cosmetic look of the entire structure. Now, it had slipped in as a parallel and integral part of the plan. It truly fascinated her, how one idea could lead to another. It was as if all the scattered dots were getting connected.

Amaya wasn't keen on endorsing any particular NGO or charitable institution, so donation boxes were a no-no. Instead, she incorporated that element by keeping and using their products. The bookmarks were at a nominal cost of five rupees. The earnings from their sale and that of the other products would be sent to an NGO support. So would the books that would make their way to the 'share a book' box.

'Slow books'—a collection of all time classics and must-reads—was being added, along with a description of the caption and a 'read more' board defining the whole concept of 'slow movement'.

After wrapping the scan and progress report of the site, Raina and she headed back to her room. Amaya got the kettle going for some green coffee and they went over the logo designs for the signboard. They considered the various options of the eye-catching colour schemes. She had sent the options across to her parents, Mihir, Anahita, Nikhil, Piya and Noor as well.

She checked her phone randomly and saw a missed call followed by a text from Rohan a little over two hours back.

'Hey, grab a copy of *Architecture Today,* like NOW!'

'Your wish is my command.'

She typed back.

She sent off her driver to get a copy and soon she was staring at the write-up on page 44.

Upcoming, young and dynamic architect Rohan Kashyap of 'Cutting Edge' has bagged the deal which collaborates the international chain of luxury serviced apartments, Bridgewater Homes, with India's leading restaurant chain VBI (Virat Bakshi Investments), to bring to India up-market corporate serviced and furnished apartments in the heart of the city. The venture will have its first construction in Mumbai, followed by Delhi, Bengaluru and Chennai. Virat Bakshi, CEO, VBI, considers this to be a breakthrough in the service industry. 'In these times, where more and more people are working in cities other than their domicile, these apartments will provide the homes they miss and yet give them the luxury of coming back to a place where all their needs are taken care of. We are fortunate to be the chosen one to get this collaboration into the country and extremely proud to do so by bringing on board this brilliant, young architect who will help us to fulfil our dream project'.

Furthermore, there was a quote from Rohan—'This is a dream

come true. We bring to India a revolutionary yet simple concept which I'm certain will quite literally find its space.'

Amaya was overjoyed for Rohan, yet completely stunned by the revelation of Rohan's other half in the project. She certainly hadn't seen that one coming! She took a couple of minutes to process this unexpected new development, deliberating on whether to bring Rohan up-to-date about her 'association' with Virat. Ratiocinating had always helped her, and she came out of this one with clarity: NO.

She made a video call to Rohan. Amaya was enthusiastically nodding her head in admiration as he came on the line.

'Well! Say something!' he exclaimed.

'You did it! I knew you would!'

'Amaya, this is the biggest thing I've ever done in my entire life! It's a huge step forward.'

'It's going to be all good, dude,' she reassured him, feeling the trepidation in his voice.

'The way you say it always works. Makes me believe it will.'

'One milestone covered, lesser miles to go...'

'So, now you get it? Why I couldn't reveal too much? I couldn't! Too much at stake.'

'Of course I do.'

'This dude, Virat Bakshi, he's a Delhi big shot!' Rohan said and she was glad she had prepared her reactions and responses.

'Yup! I know him,' Amaya said with a smile.

'You do? He seems like a cool guy. You know him well?'

'Yeah, he's cool. Umm... kind of. I know both him and his wife. You know, the extended social circle...'

'Okay...'

'So, now what? When does the project take off?'

'We're scheduled to start by next month. I need some timeout! This one's driven me crazy.'

'Do that then! Take off somewhere.'

'Wanna come along? Let's get out for a short break.'

'I still haven't covered the miles I need to here…you know how it's been with the bookstore. I can't leave it even for a day.'

'Yeah, I'm sure it's looking just the way you've envisioned it. Keep on it, girl. Maybe I'll fly in for a day or so and see what you've been up to.'

'What more could I ask for?'

'Hey, it's VB. Gotta go…talk soon.' He gestured a kiss to her and it was over and out. Amaya guessed he had received a call from Virat Bakshi.

Talk of alignment of the stars! This one was a celestial blooper. Just when Amaya was all set to give Virat the big snub, this had happened. Time to fasten the seat belt. It sure was going to be a bumpy ride ahead.

Home alone, she was wishing she could be with Rohan, a feeling that was now constant to her.

'So, I hope the mood is celebratory tonight! And if you're popping the bubbly, save some for me!'

She texted him.

'Nah! No bubbly without you! But, yeah, the party is on. The gang here won't let me go without that!'

'You deserve to celebrate!'

'Babe, I wish you were here with me.'

'I am…just a text away.'

'I don't even want you to be a millimetre away. Text miles are way too much.'

Before anything more could be said, the chat ended abruptly

ended as it usually did.

'The gang's here, gotta go…later.'

'Have fun, and send me pics…'

The man obliged her with a photo an hour later. He was looking hot, happy and high—all the right elements.

'That's MY man! Your hot lips are where I want mine to be… xx'

It was done! It was sent…without any fine print. It was bold and clearly professing her affection for him. The reaction was something that wasn't unusual when it concerned Rohan, yet one she wasn't ever prepared for—no reply! For the next two hours, she didn't get anything back from Mumbai, and as she was finally turning in, Amaya punched another one.

'Looks like the party's rocking. Save those lips for me…'

It was only the next day late afternoon that she got a response.

'Yeah, it rocked… I was smashed. Left my phone at Guy's place, just got it back…'

'Do you do that often? Leave your phone at her place?'

Amaya texted back, wanting to know more.

'Nah! This was a first. Was way too wasted! Slept at Guy's.'

'Aah! The party continued at Guy's place, eh?'

'Some of us did! Too much euphoria! Gotta love her! She made the evening what it was.'

Okay, so this puzzle solving didn't seem to be presenting any solutions. 'Her' man was probably someone else's last night. That was the reason why this 'friends with benefits' plan had never been agreeable to Amaya—too many loose ends. The derivative could be just about anything.

He seemed to have read her mind, yet again.

'Hold it right there, babe! Are you overthinking my spending the night at Guy's?'

'Well, it's an educated guess…'

'Amaya, you need to do something about your overthinking! Normally, I wouldn't even bother with an explanation, but since it's you, let me just state it for the record that Guy and I, we're the "friends with benefits" as per YOUR definition of the term. She's way too dear to me, so sex is clearly out of the equation! Thus, your overeducated guess is completely off the mark.'

'Glad to know.'

She was beaming ear-to-ear. He had actually bothered to explain to her this time. She couldn't help but be smug about it.

Twenty-nine

'Bangkok calling!'

'Huh?'

Amaya responded to Rohan's text.

'At the airport, babe... Sahil's getting hitched
so his bachelor's in Bkk.'

'And you must have been responsible for the apt choice of venue!'

'Hah! Unanimous decision. Plus, Guy's there on a shoot so it's gonna
be one big parteh!'

'You deserve it, dearest. Good to see you take a break from work. "Lap"
it up in Bkk!'

'You got it! Three days and nights of living La Dolce Vita...no limits!'

'That sounds overloaded!'

'Taking off...later.'

Amaya was quite certain there wouldn't be a later, much as she wished otherwise. Boys and Bangkok was a lethal combination. She knew there was no point waiting up for newsfeeds and texts.

Day 1: It would be past midnight in Bangkok and not surprisingly, Amaya hadn't heard from Rohan. It was a good thing she had a lot on her plate which helped her keep her mind off Rohan, even though that was a difficult thing to achieve. Knowing him, he must have switched places with the bartender. And that being the case, multitasking with texting and spinning cocktails wouldn't mix; hence communicating with him would be postponed to the following day.

Day 2: A text appeared at seven in the evening.

> 'What a party! I haven't been sober since I got here.'

'But that was the plan, wasn't it?'

> 'I wish you were here; you know how to handle drunk me.'

That was one ego massage! The man was thinking of her in a space where there was enough to keep him distracted.

'I'm sure there are many around to "manhandle" you…and I don't think you're complaining.'

> 'Oh yeah! Spoilt for choices. Guy's here too with her entourage.'

'Hmmm…sexy entourage?'

> 'Well, her friend's playing a small role in the movie, and she's here with us now. And boy, she is sexy! And hitting on me big time.'

'Oh! I thought it was just about doing it Bangkok-style…didn't realize Mumbai was also competing.'

> 'The more the merrier, babe.'

'Keep on it.'

She was getting a bad feeling about 'Mumbai and co.' It was one thing that he was on a bachelor binge, but the dynamics would change if the self-indulgence went beyond random. Amaya tried not to stress over it; he was entitled to having a 'wild time' and that was probably all there was to it.

Day 3: Amaya was all pins and needles, something she didn't remember feeling in a long time. There was no word from Rohan and she didn't want to message. It was so strange that even though they gave complete access to each other in their lives, there was hesitation when she really and truly needed to connect with him. There were 'rights to admission reserved' when it came to his personal space, not that Rohan had ever alluded so, but it was just a by-product of her overthinking mind. There wasn't much she could do about it, so she shrugged, shut that compartment and got back to the bookstore designs.

The team had incorporated Rohan's suggestions and finally, it seemed like there was a structure that could be worked upon. In fact, it was his ideas that made it move forward. She recalled her chat where she had expressed dissatisfaction and how he had goaded her into telling him what exactly she had in mind. Then, after his trip to Delhi, as promised, he'd sent her some drawings saying 'I think this is what you're looking for' and 'they are mere suggestions, not intended to undermine anybody's abilities.' When asked how he had been able to hit the nail on the head, he'd said, 'It wasn't that difficult; I heard you out and then just interpreted all you had said into plans incorporating my knowledge of you and what you'd like.' There! He had made it all sound so easy. She had tactfully worked on them, and it had worked.

Amaya was completely immersed in her work all day, but her mind drifted to Rohan on her way home. Unable to stop herself any longer, she messaged him.

'I won't be surprised if you decide to migrate to Bangkok!'

She heard back from him only the next evening. She had had an uneasy night with him constantly on her mind.

'Hey! The thought did cross my mind.'

'Why am I not surprised? How was it?'

'Excessive!'

'Tell me more.'

'Let your imagination run wild…and it still won't cover it all…'

'Rohan? Tell me.'

'Babe, like I said, anything and everything you can think of… happened.'

'Everything?'

'Yup! She was too hot to handle. She came on so strong, I was powerless.'

'And by "she" I'm assuming you mean the "actress"?'

'Yep. Niharika.'

Before she could take charge of her feelings, she helplessly punched.

'Well good for you, Mr Player. Nicely done.'

It was a good thing that texts could not convey tones because Rohan read this in a completely different one.

'Hardly a player, but learning the game…'

Amaya didn't want to communicate her angst via text. How could she? There was no basis for it. Rohan had kept sentiments completely out of their equation, and she realized that even accountability had either conveniently or assumedly been omitted. She had been so conscious of not getting too clingy knowing his phobia of the emotion-heavy zone. Without doubt, they had come a long way together but their thought processes with regard to their 'relationship' were clearly in disagreement.

It might have been a game changer for her, but apparently the texting, sexting, and baring mind, body and soul to each other didn't really qualify for a change of relationship status for Rohan. Unable to think clearly, she went back to the phone.

'Quite the sportsman I'd say! Collecting your trophies…'

'Trophies? Interesting choice of word. Never really saw it that way but trust you to do so.'

'Well, a player does collect trophies, doesn't he? And you are one helluva player!'

'Is that sarcasm I'm detecting? And here I thought I was capable of getting only one "asm" out of you.'

'You are gifted in that way…and obviously it's not just out of me that you are successful at bringing it out.'

'Whoa! Nasty.'

'More like reality.'

'What's with you, babe? Is this bad timing?'

'It's perfect timing! Game set match!'

'Okayyy…I'm not quite getting the drift.'

'That's just it Rohan, you never do get it. Or maybe you choose not to.'

Her phone rang. It was Rohan.

'What's going on with you? Is everything all right?'

'Couldn't be better.'

'Amaya, will you tell me what's on your mind? You've never been like this.'

'Just another side to me; sorry if it isn't a pretty one.'

'You know that doesn't matter to me.'

'Then enlighten me, Rohan, what does matter to you?'

'What kind of a weird question is that? You know more than anyone else what does and doesn't matter.'

'Yeah, I do, don't I? After all, I do have the consolation prize of being your preferred choice.'

'What the fuck?'

'Oh, was that presumptuous of me? I'm just a random trophy, is it?'

'You are not random...you NEVER were.'

'And now, the biggest cliché of all—I thought what you and I share is special.'

'But it is, and you know that. C'mon, you don't expect me to keep saying that to you all the time. It is a given. That's what makes you different, Amaya, what makes us different. We don't need to give each other reassurances.'

'Where is the "us" Rohan? I don't see it. All I can see is you and me.'

'In a space called us...you know that. Where are you going with all this? What's bitten you today?'

Amaya was silent for a while and realized that she was going to literally have to spell it out.

'Hey, you there?'

His voice was anxious.

'Rohan, I can't and won't be one of your many. That's where I'm going with all this. Don't worry, there isn't going to be any filmy drama, and since you're smart you must have got the drift by now.'

'Yep! I get it. I get it loud and clear.'

'That's it then. I've said what I had to.' She laughed trying to release the tension. 'You know, I can never mince my words.'

'And you don't need to with me.'

Another pregnant pause and she went on. 'All right then dude, you get on with whatever you have lined up and so will I.'

'Uh, okay. Later, then?'

'Bye, Rohan.'

Uh-oh! Bad move. The calm, composed, über-cool Amaya Kapoor should not have let herself go in this flow. All the while, she had it totally under control, but voila! She had fallen for him, plain and simple. No amount of sugarcoating could change that beat of the heart. It was emotions and mush all the way— the same predictable format that didn't change whether one was thirteen or thirty. She had probably seen it coming, but it would've been better if she had kept it to herself. There had been no need to make Rohan party to the conversation with her heart.

It was too late; she had laid the cards on the table. And that too, over a phone call. Really, there were better ways to demonstrate such theatrics. The uncomplicated had just gotten complicated—both with words and feelings. Poor chap! He must be wondering what had just hit him. But of course, he was a player, playing the field. No sympathies for him. She had just conceded out of the competition, and was aware that the ride ahead would be one emotional rollercoaster ride. It seemed her pain threshold had become inversely proportional to her increasing age. That familiar heartache was back and that too, with a bang!

Thirty

Piya was giving her the I-told-you-so look.

'You think you are one superwoman, don't you? How does it feel to be human? I mean, you get involved with a virtual stranger, give me the sales pitch about how this isn't like other relationships, blah. Well, I didn't buy it even then. Amaya, when it comes to matters of the heart, we will always be old school.'

'Yeah, I know, I know, it's your I-told-you-so moment. I screwed up. Just didn't see this one coming. It must be me. My choice of men sucks! First, I hooked up with Tarun, which was a complete fiasco and then, out of nowhere, how the direction changed to Rohan, I don't even know. He came into my life so unassumingly, was just a lad who amused me through the word games. This one's caught me totally off-guard, Piya. How could I have let this happen to me?'

'So, what now?'

'Good question! No clue. Just going to let it rest. Clear my head and think straight.'

'Maybe virtual boy will come around.'

'Don't see that happening. He's very clear about the terms and conditions for someone to be there in his life space. It was I who thought differently; I let him make an entry into my life unconditionally. Maybe it was always just in my head, this whole affection thing. We often see what we want to believe. Maybe this is what I wanted to believe—that Rohan and I were "in a space called us…"'

She looked bewildered. Piya was quiet and patiently listening to Amaya. For her to be able to process the situation, she had to let her speak.

After being lost in random thoughts for a few moments, Amaya shook herself out of the contemplation. 'It won't work out that way, and if you can't beat them, join them. So, I've added my own little "conditions apply" clause.'

'And you're worried that he might just rescind the contract?'

'Well, if he won't, I will! I mean, maybe we'll work out an agreement where we're back in the friend zone. I don't like this Piya. Maybe that's what he wanted from the start? Just sex.

'And she finally wakes up and smells the tequila!'

'But why did I expect anything more? Why did I not grasp this better?'

The thought that Rohan's agenda was clear from the start and she had her blinders on made her feel sick. All this bullshit about him not having an 'agenda', that he couldn't handle emotional spookiness was just that—BULLSHIT; she had bought it all. It had all been working accordingly to his plan but now this minor glitch was a spoiler alert. Piya, however, thought she was overreacting.

'C'mon Amu, I'm not a huge fan of the guy, but nah, you're way off the mark here. I don't think he'd make all this effort just for a lay, to add you to his collectibles, as you say. He's got it all going for him. I mean to think YOU have fallen for him, would make him a piece of work. It's pretty simple, he's in 'no strings attached mode' and you aren't. This is just a mini-personal disaster. So, stop running yourself down, give that vodka to your soul, keep your chin up and be fabulous, like you always are. You can handle yourself and your tipsy heart girl, you know that.'

📖

Mihir. She wondered how he would react to all this, what with Rohan and he seeming to be on the same plane when it came to the 'friends with benefits' strategy. He would probably endorse Piya's view, underplay the situation; tell her it was her choice and if she had made one, she should stick by it and not expect the other party to toe the line. Since he himself never gave serious consideration to monogamy, he would preach what he practised. One call to him and he could sense he was on duty. They met later that evening and talked it out.

'I need to get drunk tonight.'

'And you should. I'm always your partner in crime.' Mihir handed her the iced vodka-soda-lime. She downed it quickly and started on the second one. The third followed soon.

'I'm in trouble, Mihir. I've fallen hard. It's the right guy, wrong timing or is it the wrong guy, wrong timing? He's perfect and yet so imperfect. What's with you men? Why can't the love of one good woman be enough for you all?' High and babbly, she let herself go.

'We're greedy like that. We want it all,' Mihir said without a moment's hesitation.

'And one woman can't be that "ALL"?'

'Be fair, Amaya. How does the man know that this is what you've been thinking while your actions are completely in the bindaas mode? He's riding smoothly with you, and all of sudden, you change the lane. He didn't see it coming, sweetheart.'

'I didn't see it coming, Mihir. I don't even remember the last time I was so cut up about a man. After Gautam, there's been no one. But, this time...' she frowned.

'Give him a chance, Amaya, let him also process what's going on.'

'I can't play mind games and you know it. I always say it like it is, and that's just what I've done. I'm not going to be one of his many.'

Mihir gave her the 'commitment resistant' guy's perspective. He himself was oscillating between Noor and Raina. It was a situation he was comfortable with and he had made it clear to both the women. Amaya argued, saying that her take was different. Without wanting to sound judgemental, she said that she was neither Raina nor Noor, adding that she wasn't hankering after a commitment; she herself wasn't ready for one. At the same time, she couldn't have him play the field and she needed to make that very clear to him, since he clearly, was on a different drift.

It was messy and Amaya wasn't a happy girl. She'd had a long day, an emotionally trying one at that. A good night's sleep and probably a clearer head in the morning was all she was praying for. Work the next morning had all the makings of a crazy day. Amaya wanted to put the Rohan chapter on hold and dive deep into work.

The next meeting would be a toughie. Tarun was coming in for the final touches of the book dummy before it was sent to press. Despite his efforts, she had not taken their personal encounter any further than that one night. In due course, he had gotten the message. She hoped he would be his usual professional self. She was already emotionally drained and didn't have the patience to handle another soppy situation. Fortunately, her assistant and the event management team would be part of the session.

Tarun steered clear of any personal talk and Amaya

respected that. In fact, he was his witty self and they had a pleasant brainstorming session regarding his book launch. He was already onboard with the book-tasting plan on Facebook and Twitter, which had been her suggestion, and complimented her on it being bang on as he hadn't anticipated the reach of the medium. She laughed and told him that 'social media' was no longer just a medium; it was a phenomenon and he agreed. Once he left, Amaya wondered why destiny had steered her away from this cracker of a writer towards the most unlikely candidate. The last few months had been only about Rohan, with no other man crossing her mind. God must have a plan!

Thirty-one

Amaya was on a flight to Mumbai. Guy had gotten in touch with her saying that Rajbir was back in town after his two-month shooting stint overseas. She had also confirmed that Mega Books had made an offer but he was yet to take a final decision. Putting in a word for Amaya Books, Guy had fixed a meeting between Amaya and the reclusive director-producer. Knowing how persuasive Meghna Roy could be, she didn't want to lose another moment in trying to take over this deal. She worked out the strategy in her head. She wasn't going to bring up Mega Books or her knowledge of the goings-on. She would just make an aggressive case for why it was a good idea for Rajbir Singh's memoirs to be an Amaya Books' publication.

'Mr Rajbir Singh. Pleasure. Amaya Kapoor.' Amaya stretched her hand while walking into his room in the bustling office at a suburban studio.

'Rajbir will do just fine, Amaya,' he said smilingly with a firm handshake. He gestured for her to take a seat and sat across her. He was even more slender than he looked in the couple of photographs that the media circulated over and over again, given that there wasn't much fodder on him to print. They made small talk for a while before Amaya got to the point.

'Being a publisher and well aware of the current market trends, I believe this is the perfect time for your memoir to hit the market. The industry is on an upswing. You have an amazing career and repertoire of films under your banner. It would be an absolute bestseller. It would be a personal honour if you consider Amaya Books as your prospective publisher.' He looked somewhat older than his fifty years. Gaunt and thin with salt-and-pepper hair, he could easily be looked over in a crowd, but the glint in his eyes reflected the passion and zeal this big gun was renowned for—not just in India but also internationally.

'Yes, I am in the process. But I'm an amateur writer.'

'This is your debut as an author. Yes, writing a full-length book is somewhat different from scripting but at heart, it is all about the art of writing. If you have the basic material down we will be able to help you polish it up and bring it on a level that will mirror the kind of writing that you are known for.'

'It is true that I've led an eventful life. There's a lot to tell, a lot to talk about and disclose. And I'm ready to do it now.'

'And that is precisely the heart of a memoir. It needs to have a "behind the scenes" in it. And like you said, you have a prodigious life story to tell.'

'It may raise a controversy or two. I plan on telling almost all.'

'Controversial is good. Sensationalism is not. I'm sure you'll agree with me. I want to take you in the right direction and not mislead you in any way just to sell an extra few copies. That said, I want to let the world know that the man behind the larger-than-life celluloid canvasses and dreamy romances is real. And his life is no less than that.'

'I like you, Amaya. I like the honesty, the no-nonsense approach. The other day, another lady was here. I'm not going to take names but she... The way she put things, I just wasn't convinced that it was the right place to send my story.'

Amaya acted ignorant to the info-byte provided to her.

'Rajbir, you'll have many more and bigger bids. No doubting that. All I can assure you is Amaya Books will make your book just what you want it to be; we will hold your hand editorially and in every other department, but the heart of the book will remain yours. We know what works and what doesn't. And I get the feeling, as I hope you do, that putting our heads and minds together will result in an awe-inspiring, coming-of-age book.'

Amaya was pleased with her pitch, and she believed and practised that philosophy. She was quite certain Rajbir Singh was convinced.

Amaya had messaged Rohan just before taking off from Delhi. They planned to meet for a quick coffee at a suburban café on her way back to the airport. Amaya was all set for the bravado. For the life of him, Rohan wouldn't be able to tell what was in her mind and heart. He gave her a warm hug and asked about her meeting. She said it had gone well, after which Rohan inquired about the bookstore.

'It's looking great, Rohan,' she told him enthusiastically. 'We open next month. All the things you had told me about the open space—that's what it's going to be. We've planned cookouts, art and photography exhibitions, workshops, all lined up.'

'Good on you. You've done it,' Rohan said, his voice filled with admiration. And then he asked, 'Amaya, are we cool?'

'Absolutely. We are totally cool.'

'Then why haven't I heard from you in a long time?'

'I could say the same to you. It takes two to tango. I'm always a text away when you need me. That hasn't changed.'

'Then what has?' he asked.

She was quiet. She took a few sips of her coffee, deliberating on where to take the conversation.

'C'mon, Rohan. We've had the talk. We're friends. That's not going to change. However, our definitions of the term differ. The ones you want to derive out of yours don't work for me— you know that.' She smiled, trying to steer the conversation to a lighter direction.

'I miss you Amaya. I miss talking to you. But if this is what you want, then that's what it will be.' He said in a tone that Amaya found difficult to decode.

'Let's not get into what I or you want.' Before he could add anything else, she called for the cheque and said, 'Shall we? I need to get to the airport.' They were walking out of the crowded café towards the cab when Rohan said, 'What if I want to kiss you right now?' with an emphasis on the words 'right' and 'now'. His eyes were gleaming with desire and he had the look that Amaya had seen time and again. That did it for her. Something in her just snapped. It was as if he hadn't been listening to a word she'd said. Not giving a rat's ass to their surroundings, she turned to him, pulled him closer and gave him a full-mouthed kiss that he responded to passionately. Cocking her head to one side, Amaya smiled and said, 'Happy?'

Before he could react, she said, 'Gotta catch that flight now. You take care of yourself.' She didn't wait for the reaction and sat in the cab.

The kiss felt good, as they all had since their first one in Mumbai. But that was no longer enough. Rohan Kashyap would never understand where she was coming from, or maybe he just didn't want to. He was wired differently. And that was why she had done what she did. Amaya Kapoor wasn't going to beg for affection from anyone. She had indulged him far too much already. And now, as far as he was concerned, the 'friends' and 'benefits' territories would be clearly demarcated in her life and there wouldn't be any overlapping.

Thirty-two

*F*inally! It was the day of reckoning. The day Amaya Books and More would be launched. Amaya's vision had translated into something solid and was up for all to see. Now, it was her instinct versus a world in which a book was just 'a click away'.

Over two hundred guests, including friends, family and professional contacts, would be at the launch in the evening. Raina and she had been planning the event for a month, designed to be a simple, classy affair that would present the bookstore to the city.

Anahita had flown in for her sister's big day. Both siblings were the first ones to arrive at 6.30 p.m. and that gave Amaya a prep time of half an hour. She had picked a sleeveless knee-length navy blue dress that was fitted at the waist and flared below. Teamed with a pair of small but noticeable diamond earrings and basic pumps, it was the typical 'Amaya' look.

Both the ladies took a final look of the ground floor before the guests arrived. The part-kitschy, part-modern interiors had been a tough combination to pull off but Amaya was glad that she hadn't settled for second best. One wall in each of the three rooms was offset with funky wallpaper and the rest three with a sundried brick look; it provided the perfect balance to the décor. The painting she had picked from Oakland stood tall on the wall of the reading lounge. The backdrop behind the cashier had a mock bookshelf with books and quotes by well-known writers. A circular wall clock was placed on one corner. All over the store, the brick walls were visible through the bookshelves.

Amaya took Anahita to the shelf that was titled 'Slow Books' where a hand-picked collection of all-time classics and must-reads was placed. It held a carefully picked selection of books that one could read over and over again. Her folks had loved the concept and thought it fit very well in the store. It had come out looking very cool, Amaya thought to herself, reading the board that defined the entire philosophy of 'slow movement'. 'This one's for you, Anirudh,' she said out aloud. It truly did belong to him. She told Anahita that she was convinced that meeting Anirudh had been part of a bigger plan—to bring that section to the bookstore. It was something deeper than just a coincidence. Anahita took pictures of the same to send to Anirudh. After a quick scan of the first floor that housed the kids' section and the café, they returned to the garden.

Neena and Anand Kapoor were already there along with Raina. 'Mom, the benches were such a great idea,' Anahita said. Neena had insisted on getting the benches painted in bright colours and had placed them randomly in the garden, for readers to hang around during Delhi winters and cool evenings. They would make for perfect seating for the events too. The 'Chai ka Thela' or tea cart, stood in one corner of the garden. The paint and artwork was coordinated with the benches. The entire expanse looked thoroughly inviting to any reader.

'Raina! You look gorgeous!' Amaya said. She was indeed looking stunning in a plain black saree and gold embroidered sleeveless blouse. Raina had put her heart, soul and mind into the project. Even then, she was overseeing the last-minute details. Amaya's decision to indict her into the schematic had breathed new life into Raina.

'We're on, Amaya! I can't thank you enough for this,' Raina said, with a bit of a tremble in her voice that Amaya caught on to.

'Back at you, girl! We're a kickass team and don't you forget that,' Amaya said. The opportunity had worked well for Raina. She was piecing her life together, taking on the challenges and delivering results. Sometimes all one needed was that one chance to make all the wrongs, right. Amaya was glad to have been the giver. Raina and Anahita caught up over a quick chit-chat.

Mihir was already on the job as the official photographer for the event.

'This is going to be my haunt in the days to come. Thank you, Amaya, for giving Delhi ABM!'

She hugged him with an 'Amen.' Raina and he whispered something to each other. Mihir and Raina continued to be 'great together' and Amaya thought it was best to leave it at that. She had been unable to solve the Noor-Mihir-Raina algorithm.

She passed the open courtyard in the centre of the store. It was visible through the closed glass walls from within the store. It would be used as an alternate exhibit area during the bad weather months where unbearable heat and rain would make it impossible to enjoy the outdoors.

Amaya had sent Rohan an official invite for the opening. He had confirmed by saying he knew it was one of the most important days of her life and he would most definitely be a part of it.

'Waiting to see ABM! And you! I miss you, Amaya…'

'You asked for it.'

'I haven't asked for anything…yet. Your "overthinking" has made me miss you.'

'You didn't leave me with any other choice.'

'And here I thought I was the chosen one.'

'Again…you chose to undo this.'

'Fuck you!'

'You did…real bad.'

The whole text exchange had been so ill-humoured, which was a rarity compared to their otherwise vibrant conversations. Amaya had ended up sounding like a cranky, silly girl. It was just as well that Rohan hadn't replied to her last line. She would not have either, had she been in his place.

It had taken her 'all' to keep from texting him ever since, but it had to stop. And it had. The 'textpectations', the many moments of communication with Rohan had added so much more to her life. Come to think of it, they had been the basis of their 'relationship'. The to and fro of those engaging, unusual and exhilarating texts had become so addictive that she had gone through a period of withdrawal where she had to use her willpower to resist punching one to him. Now she was waiting for him to arrive, not knowing whether he would at all, and apprehensive on how she'd meet him if he did. Amaya sighed and turned her attention to greeting her guests.

'Meghna Roy did decide to grace the occasion after all,' Amaya thought to herself. She looked stunning in a blue and red Pakistani ensemble. She always managed to get the look right. Her dad was already greeting Meghna and Sharad as Amaya walked towards them.

'Meghna, thank you so much for being here today,' Amaya said and then greeted Sharad.

'I wouldn't have missed it for anything, Amaya! You've

managed another ace up your sleeve. This bookstore is quite a surprise,' said Meghna, her tone laced with an obvious mix of admiration and envy.

'No dearth of surprises, Meghna. Watch the space for more,' Amaya beamed.

She spotted Virat and Rupali. Rupali greeted her coldly and walked ahead. She wondered why the usually over-friendly Rupali had met her thus. But before she could dwell on it any further, Virat embraced Amaya and squeezed her hand in his usual inappropriate gesture.

'It's been a while, Amaya! I'm getting tired of the chase.'

'And how is that my problem, Virat?' she asked him with a smile so as to not give away any part of the conversation to those around them. It was incredulous of him to bring this up at that moment. Virat looked surprised. Before the conversation could go any further, the next guest made them both turn around.

'Virat! Good to see you here, man,' Rohan shook hands with him and turned to Amaya. 'You did it finally.' He said with admiration after giving her a hug.

'I'm glad you're here,' Amaya said to him.

'And why would I not be? Not a chance that I'd miss being around for your big moment, Retro.' The remark was to melt her heart. She gave him a warm smile.

'So, you two know each other?' said Virat.

'Yeah, and it seems you do too, Virat?'

'Oh yes, we go back a long way. What about you?' he asked Rohan.

'Hasn't been that long for us but who's to say where we go from here? Maybe a long way forward, what do you say, Amaya?' He smiled at her. In an attempt to not show her puzzlement at that sphinx of a statement, Amaya changed the topic. 'You two have a fantastic venture coming up.'

'Ah. You're well updated then. Yeah, he's my golden-eyed boy. We have great hopes from him.' Virat said, patting Rohan on his shoulder. 'Let's drink to that, shall we?' Amaya left the two to their devices and went to greet her other guests who had just arrived.

And in walked Tarun and Noor. 'When did this happen?' was the question she had for Noor as she met them both, trying not to look shocked. Tarun was a closed chapter for Amaya and vice versa. But did this mean Noor and Mihir were history, too? Or was Tarun just another angle that converted the triangle into a quadrilateral?

'We need to talk!' Amaya whispered to Noor who nodded in agreement.

'He's here?' Piya didn't hide her surprise when Amaya told her about Rohan's arrival. 'I don't know what to make of it, Amaya. But where is he? I want to meet him now!'

Anahita nodded in unison.

She introduced Anahita, Piya and Atul to Rohan and left them in each other's company. The media was present in full swing and she left the job of handling the PR to Raina. Amaya posed for a few photographs but not before telling the camerapersons to focus on the bookstore as that was what the evening was all about. She spotted many guests who were doing the rounds of the store, stopping at places of their interest.

As the evening went on, Amaya happened to look in the direction of Noor and Tarun. Tarun was mushy with his women, she knew that about him. He loved to fawn and fuss around them like a lost puppy. And that was what he was doing with Noor who seemed to be enjoying every bit of the attention. In what was an involuntary action, Amaya looked at Mihir and found him staring at them. His expression was a mixture of jealousy and curiosity. She shook her head in amusement. Men and their vanity! Mihir probably couldn't get over the fact that Noor could finally see beyond him.

Thirty-three

The next guest walked in with fanfare. Amaya had been eagerly awaiting his arrival. She had sent a senior staffer to fetch him from the airport. He almost hadn't made it, owing to the delayed fight, but was she glad he was finally here! She rushed across the garden to welcome him. And without further ado, she grabbed the mic and said, 'Attention everyone! I hope you all are enjoying Amaya Books and More.' All eyes and ears turned towards her. Amaya's eyes in turn moved from Rohan who was giving her a silent applaud, to Meghna Roy.

'We have another proud announcement to make today. Please let's hear it for the internationally renowned and critically acclaimed director, RAJBIR SINGH.' Her dad was beaming with pride. She continued, looking directly at Meghna, 'Amaya Books is soon to publish the much-awaited memoir of the man himself.'

Saying this, she handed the mic to Rajbir. 'Well, all I can say is that if anyone could convince me to write this book, it was Amaya!'

Meghna looked devastated, as if she'd been hit by a truck. The usually articulate Ms Roy couldn't hide her astonishment and displeasure. She walked out of the party in a huff with Sharad following her. Amaya didn't make an attempt to stop her. She had imagined that this coup would strike Meghna down, but hadn't quite expected such an extreme reaction.

Rohan was by her side. 'And she does it again!' he said to her, his eyes gleaming with admiration. She introduced him to Rajbir saying that the two had a friend in common—Gayatri. Rajbir was all praises for her. He was soon surrounded by many guests wanting selfies with him. He was a shy and reticent man and Amaya could tell he was having difficulty handling the attention. 'It takes all kinds,' Amaya thought. Any other 'Bollywood' celeb would be used to the limelight and would gladly oblige the takers.

After taking a quick but appreciative round of the store, Rajbir took leave, saying he had an early morning flight to catch. Amaya, her folks and Anahita saw him to the gate, and Anahita went on and on about how she was a fan of his movies. She, too, took a selfie with him before he finally left.

'Amaya! Whatever happened to Meghna? She's left already?' Anand asked his daughter.

'Seems so, Dad.'

'Strange! That's not like her at all.'

'Yeah, I think she wasn't too happy with us bagging Rajbir!'

'Not again, Amaya,' said Neena. 'She was pitching for this one too? What is it with the two of you?'

'Don't know, Mom. I do seem to be rubbing her the wrong way off late,' she winked at her mom. As she kept greeting and chatting with the guests, her mind was still on Meghna. Her reaction had been unexpected. It was not like her to make her feelings so obvious.

'Amaya, Rajan and gang want a tour of the bookstore.' Anand Kapoor pulled her out of her abstraction.

'Sure, Dad.'

She led the bunch through the ground to the first floor, chatting along the way and answering their queries. Finding a free moment as the rest of the lot moved back downstairs,

Amaya moved for the restroom. As she fixed her hair and face, she couldn't stop smiling. Oh! The look on Meghna Roy's face had been worth all the effort she had made to convince Rajbir. He had sent her a mail within a month of her return from Mumbai, stating his desire to go with Amaya Books. They had spoken to each other the very next day.

'Hi Rajbir! This is going to be one hell of a book. When can you send me the manuscript?' she asked him. They had gone on to discuss deadlines and firming up publishing schedules. Amaya knew this was going to be a massive project and it would be a super opportunity to have incredible sales in the international market too.

On her way out from the restroom, she saw Rupali standing right in front of her. 'Hey, all yours,' she said, assuming that Rupali too wanted to make use of it.

'All mine? Or all yours?' said Rupali, taking a swig of the wine.

'Huh?'

'Don't act coy, you bitch. I know you're coming onto him. I saw you both at that party. I saw the way you look at him. I KNOW EVERYTHING!' said Rupali, raising her pitch.

'You're way off, Rupali. Calm down. Ask Virat. He'll tell you that you've got it all wrong.'

The drama was the last thing Amaya needed.

'Then let's call him right away.'

Before Amaya could say anything further, Rupali made a call, 'Virat baby, could you come upstairs for a minute?'

Amaya didn't want this getting out of hand. Rupali downed the remaining wine and was about to say something when Virat arrived.

'What's going on, Rupali? Amaya?' he asked them both.

Rupali turned to Virat. 'I saw everything that night. The

two of you on the dance floor.' Then directing her accusatory gaze at Amaya, she continued, 'You thought you could get away with it, huh?' I've known since then that there's something going on between you two.'

Virat moved next to her and said, 'Oh sweetheart! That was nothing.' He gestured to Amaya. 'She was drunk and got carried away. You know how it is. But she's a friend and we've settled it. She's understood that, honey. Now just let it all be. Let's not spoil her moment.'

His words left Amaya dumbstruck. She was drunk? She got carried away? She wanted to correct him right then but Rupali was unstoppable.

'To hell with her moment. Amaya, how dare you? You stay away from him, you hear me? And don't move from here till you settle this once and for all.'

'What the fuck, Virat? I piled on to you?' Amaya said.

Resisting her intense urge to slap Virat across his face, she tried to calm herself down. This was bad timing. She couldn't let go of herself, not here, not right now. Virat the 'Superstud' had just turned into Virat the 'wuss'! He was holding Rupali, like her little lamb.

'Hey, I thought the party was downstairs,' came a voice from behind. The three turned around at once. It was Rohan, to add to the chaos.

Amaya's eyes met Rohan's and then they pointed to Virat. He acknowledged the gesture with an affirmative nod. Such was the understanding between them. Rohan figured out that the anonymous married man in all her references was none other than Mr Bakshi.

'Amaya, do you want to settle this?' he said with the usual tilt of the head. He then shrugged his shoulders with his characteristic smile. She guessed he had heard some part of the conversation, if not all.

'Rohan, you needn't be a part of this.' Amaya didn't want to jeopardize his professional connection with Virat. It was a sticky situation and she had to slip out of it without any glitches, at least for now.

Rohan ignored Amaya's comment and continued, 'You're absolutely right, Mrs Bakshi! Amaya goes nowhere till she tells you exactly what she's been telling Virat all these days. That he doesn't need to be anywhere near her. Babe, do the needful please, right now.'

His voice was stern and protective.

Amaya looked at Virat and said as calmly as she could, 'Virat, this would be a good time for you take Rupali home.'

'Yeah, Virat. Would be a good idea to give Mrs Bakshi the whole picture on how wrong she is in her deduction about Amaya and you.'

Virat was staring at Rohan, trying to figure where he fit in in all this. Rupali was a mess. She was tipsy and beside herself. 'You stay away from him!' she slurred and gave Amaya a slight push.

'She will! Gladly!' Rohan held Amaya from behind. She was in his arms and he came by her side and held her hand. 'Virat, you should get going. I'm sure you understand how off the timing is. This is a bookstore launch, it is business, and personal matters can be dealt with later.'

Without saying anything further, Virat took hold of the mumbling Rupali and exited. Amaya didn't have the luxury to dwell over all that had just transpired. It had happened too quickly—Rupali's accusations, Virat's 360-degree turn and Rohan's gallant contribution to the episode. Before she could ask him anything, Rohan said, 'Phew! You Dilliwallahs are such suckers for drama.' He made an effort to play down what had happened. And what was again typically Rohan, it was devoid of any emotion.

'Welcome to the joyrides in the amusement park called people!' she added, keeping to his drift.

'There you go again, my "wordly wise" woman.'

Amaya made note of the word 'my'.

Rohan then said, 'Might I remind you now that you have a job to do? Downstairs, shall we?'

He was right. She had to continue playing hostess for the evening. Amaya disconnected from the last few minutes and walked over to Anahita who gave her a questioning look.

'Will tell you all later,' Amaya told her concerned sibling.

Rohan whispered to her, 'You take care of your business while I explore your labour of love.'

'No, wait. Don't just yet. Let me wrap the evening and we'll do it together.'

He looked at her straight in the eye. 'I'll be waiting. It's what I'm here for.' He smiled and moved towards Mihir.

She then joined her dad and others. 'It's Amaya's vision, her conviction and concept. I can take no credit for it.' Anand Kapoor's pride was apparent.

'He's the rock behind it all. They both are,' Amaya said, nodding at her folks. The evening seemed perfect, except for the glitch with the Bakshis. The response of most present was encouraging. The concept seemed to be spot on. Where it all went from there was a wait-and-watch game. Once the guests and her folks had left, it was just Rohan and Amaya in the bookstore.

She asked, 'Ready for the tour?'

'With you as the tour guide? Always!'

They walked back inside. To the left of the entrance was a blackboard resting on an easel. It was titled 'Word of the Day' and was followed by 'Logophile (n): A lover of words'.

Rohan looked at Amaya and smiled. 'What brought about the change of heart?' He remembered that Amaya had dismissed his idea when he had first suggested it in Mumbai.

She smiled and said, 'There isn't any. It's just a change of mind.'

'That mind...' He reached out to her forehead and continued, 'It has me taken since you first trapezed into my life via that board.'

'I'm not the only one apparently. Last I knew your life was a circus with your own personal trapeze artists.'

'You aren't gonna forgive me on that one? I deserve it, I guess.'

'I don't fit in, Rohan. Your life space is too crowded for me. I thrive more on exclusive rights of admission, you know that,' she said as they walked to the next room.

'Yeah I've been thinking about that,' he said. He turned to the 'Slow Books' corner and spent time on it. 'Hmmm, another winner concept, this!'

'You've been thinking?' she asked.

'What can I say? You're addictive, lady.'

'That doesn't really sound like a compliment.'

'It wasn't meant to be one. It's more of a declaration based on factual evidence.'

'What are the facts then?'

'Plain and simple. You have me exclusively. This fact good enough for you?'

'Define "exclusively".'

The word she was searching for was the one he didn't have in his dictionary. He caught on and laughed.

'Nothing can go past you, huh? Well, that word and me, we have issues—you know that. It spooks me, you know that too.'

'About time you faced your fears, Superman!'

'I would've punched that asshole in his face for what he said to you. Does that count for being "emotional"? There, I've said it!'

'I'm listening.'

'I'm ready to give it a shot.'

She stayed silent. He wanted to say more and she needed him to.

'Look, I don't know where I'm headed. This is the road less travelled for me. But I'd like you to keep me company on my way. And you can hope that there's light at the end of the tunnel.'

'Tunnels don't scare me, Rohan. Neither does the path. The only hitch in your plot is the "conditions applied" clause. Also, I'm more of a stay-connected girl and your middle name is "incommunicado".'

He turned to her and held out his right hand, gesturing a handshake.

'Consider the conditions dropped then. And Rohan Kashyap it is from now on.'

She moved her hand forward and he held on to it. He pulled her closer and wrapped his arm around her shoulders.

'That was easy.'

'That's just it, Amaya. You make it all seem so easy.'

'It's you and me, Rohan. It's US.'

'US. I like the sound of that word. Always have when you say it.'

'There's a lot more to the word than phonetics. You sure you're up for it?'

'Hell no, I'm not near fucking sure. All I know is that anything that even remotely sounds like "US" has to have you in it.' He paused and then sighed, 'Be patient with me, Amaya.'

'Patience is an inexhaustible life resource that I possess. You should know that by now.'

He moved forward to kiss her and she responded. Then he said, 'This feels better.' He tucked a stray lock behind her ears, as he normally did when they were together. 'Now let's call it a day, shall we? I've seen what I needed to see most.'

'If it were left to me, I wouldn't let you go…'

He pointed his index finger towards her. 'Hold that thought amongst the many others you're holding! I better get going. Gotta handle an angry married man tomorrow morning,' said Rohan.

'I've put you in a spot with him, haven't I? Thank you for taking up my cause on that one.'

'Yeah, he's not going to be a happy man after what I did today, but it was totally worth it! Bet the feminist in you didn't like that at all.'

'Maybe, but it wooed me completely. And I appreciated it immensely. If that was the plan, then you succeeded.'

'I didn't come with a game plan, Amaya. There aren't any agendas here,' he said, looking a bit miffed. "I've put my cards on the table. Now it's all upto you."

After a few moments of silence, she asked him, 'So what's your plan for tomorrow?'

'That would directly depend on where you take this from here. I'll deal with Mr Bakshi first thing in the morning. After which I'll decide whether I head to the airport or plan a lunch date if and when I hear from you tomorrow. Let's leave at that for now and I will be waiting with bated breath, that I assure you, muh lady!'

He gave her a peck on her cheek and left. He was right. He had made himself clear that he was ready to take their relationship to the next level. He had put forth his apprehensions and misgivings. Now, it was her turn. This would be a tough night for her to get through.

☐

'Hey, just wrapped the meeting,'

Rohan texted the next afternoon.

'How'd it go?'

'Just the way it should have.'

Amaya knew she wouldn't get any dope from him on that. It was work stuff which he hardly ever discussed with her. She felt relieved, though, that the damage had been repairable.

'You got a good night's sleep? Or let me guess. You were up thinking all night, eh?'

'Hmmm…'

'Hmmmm. How about I give you a word of the day?'

'I'm all eyes!'

'"YOURS" (pronoun): officially used to refer to a thing or things belonging to or associated with the person or people that the speaker is addressing." Here, it is used to describe me. You could apply suitable adverbs as add-ons.'

'You sure? I have a substantial list and I'm not in a mood to negotiate.'

'Since when did you become a hard taskmaster? Btw…you're the one who inspired me to be sure. Now, do we meet or do I head to the airport?'

'I'm coming to see you right away!'

'Super! Then, all I will do today is figure out meanings with you. Room 421. See you soon.'

Amaya couldn't wait to be with him. And soon enough, she was knocking at Room 421. Rohan pulled her in and they kissed. He held her tightly and continued to kiss her.

'I have something for you,' he said to her.

'Oh my God! Rohan Kashyap, do not tell me you've got me a gift! This is a first!' Amaya was shocked. This was so not the Rohan she had known.

'No way! Do not jump to predictable conclusions, wise one!' he exclaimed and then went down on his knees.

'Rohan...' Amaya was lost for a reaction. This couldn't be happening. It was out of the question. How could he even think of proposing to her? Where was this coming from? The synapses of her mind were somersaulting. Kneeling before her, Rohan put his hand in his pocket and pulled something out with his fist closed.

Still kneeling, he opened his hand in front of her. In it was a key in a leather keychain. 'Amaya Kapoor, will you accept this key to my apartment as an acknowledgement to the fact that I'm making the word "yours" official?'

'And you call me a drama queen,' Amaya smiled.

'As always, there's so much to learn from you. Well, what say?' he smiled and asked.

'You know what this means, Rohan?'

'No, not really. It isn't exactly a "been there done that" situation. But I'm willing to discover its true meaning with you. Let's do this, Amaya!'

'I don't know what to say...'

'The wordly-wise, at a loss of words? That's got to be a first!'

'It's all thanks to you. I'm completely in the red with you. The things you make me do.'

'I haven't even started on that, babe. And I too have a long list.'

Amaya took the key from his hand and Rohan got up. 'So that's settled then. How about you open a bookstore in Mumbai now?' He was already reading her mind and her concerns regarding the longitudinal distance between them.

'Now you've got me thinking again! And maybe...just maybe, I'll hire you to design it.'

'Better give that a thought. That's going to mean too much of me in your life.'

'I'm up for it,' Amaya said drifting into her thoughts, 'This... is my kairos!'

'Your what? Didn't take you long to regain the word power! Woman, can you ever speak in the lingo used by us lesser mortals?' He ran his fingers through her hair.

'I'll try. We both know how arduous a task that is for me,' she winked at him.

'You do your part and I'll do mine. Let's hit that uncharted road, babe. Welcome aboard...'

New dreams, new vistas and a man by her side.

Thrilled with what life had to offer her, Amaya Kapoor was ready to take it all onboard, one word at a time.

Acknowledgements

Writing *Great Textpectations* has been a truly gratifying journey, one which would not have been the same without the support of my Team GT:

My mother Chetana Kohli and my late father Suresh Kohli have been a source of inspiration to me all my life. Their constant encouragement, their ability and insistence to give me the roots to stay grounded and the wings to explore my space, are the very foundation that I stand on today.

My husband Aman Vadehra—my pal and most unabashed critic.

My son Anav and daughter Manya—my biggest blessings.

My sisters, Kanchi Kohli and Nupur Bery, read and reread the many versions of the draft with utmost devotion and honesty. My brother-in-law, Rishi Bery, a man of few words, saved some of the most worthy ones as feedback.

My in-laws, Sudha and Mohan Vadehra, who are my second set of parents; my brother-in-law Karan, and sister-in-law Shalini Vadehra, who, over the years, has become more of a 'sister' than the 'in-law'.

My uncle Devindra Kohli and aunt Vijaya John Kohli provided valuable insight and guidance to steer me on this path.

My friend, philosopher and guide Rohit Sethi constantly pushed me and never let me get too complacent about what I wrote, his outright faith in my writing notwithstanding.

My dear friend Punnya Vij, though much younger in the years, has given me the perspective which age and experience sometimes fall short of providing.

A big shout out to my inner circle of friends and my un-biological sisters—my girlfriends, who always, ALWAYS, have my back.

My publishers, Rupa Publications, for giving me the opportunity to now be known as 'Ruchi Vadehra, writer.'